My Very
UN
^ Fairy Tale
Life

My Very UN Fairy Tale Life

ANNA STANISZEWSKI

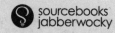

sourcebooks
jabberwocky

Published by Sourcebooks Jabberwocky, an imprint of Sourcebooks, Inc.
P.O. Box 4410, Naperville, Illinois 60567-4410
(630) 961-3900
Fax: (630) 961-2168
www.jabberwockykids.com

Library of Congress Cataloging-in-Publication data is on file with the pub-
lisher.

Source of Production: Webcom, Toronto, Canada
Date of Production: September 2011
Run Number: 16090

Printed and bound in Canada.
WC 10 9 8 7 6 5 4 3 2 1

This book belongs to*:

_____

*Disclaimer: By printing your name you hereby agree to become an Adventurer for life, and you accept the job's various benefits, rules, and dangers. You vow to help *all* creatures of the magical variety (including killer unicorns) maintain peace, order, and happiness in their respective kingdoms. **Failure to carry out your Adventurer duties will result in a disciplinary hearing before the Committee. And trust me, you *really* don't want that to happen.

**Magical gnome sidekick not included.

"*If you want your children to be intelligent, read them fairy tales. If you want them to be more intelligent, read them more fairy tales.*"

—Albert Einstein

PART 1

Chapter 1

You know all those stories that claim fairies cry sparkle tears and elves travel by rainbow? They're lies. All lies. No one tells you the truth until it's too late. And then all you can do is run like crazy while a herd of unicorns tries to kill you.

Of course, I had no idea what I'd done to get the unicorns all riled up. So much for having a magical guide to help me with my adventures. Anthony was about as useful as a bent thumbtack. Still, I needed his magic if I was going to get out of this mission alive.

"Anthony!" I shrieked as I darted down a hill and away from the stampeding unicorns. "Anthony, help me!" Where was that carrot-headed gnome?

The unicorns' glittering horns were right behind me. Another minute and I'd be a marshmallow on a stick.

"All right, Jenny," I said to myself. "You can do this." I

forced my burning legs to speed up. If I could just get far enough away, I might be able to hide.

I dashed behind a tree and pressed up against the trunk. A second later, the herd tore past at hurricane speed. But I wasn't safe for long. The unicorns screeched to a stop and whipped around to face me. Their golden eyes were tiny slits.

"Look," I said, gripping the tree trunk for support. "I was just trying to teach you guys how to share. If you want to keep fighting over that rainbow, that's your business."

The unicorn leader stepped forward. His horn was a full foot taller than all the others, and his head was decorated with tiny, bell-like flowers.

"Can't we all just get along?" I said. Cheesy sayings always popped out of my mouth during adventures, even when I didn't want them to.

"Nay," said the unicorn.

"What?"

"Nay!"

"Is that like a horse neigh or a 'no' nay?"

"Naaay!" the unicorn sputtered.

I fought back a hysterical giggle. Anthony had warned me that unicorns couldn't produce human speech, even though they could understand it. Still, I couldn't get over

4

the fact that these mythical creatures could sound so much like…well, like regular horses.

"I already tried to explain to you. I'm an adventurer," I told them. "I was sent here to help you. But clearly you don't want my help. So if you don't mind, I'd really like to get home now. My aunt's probably worried sick about me." This last part wasn't quite true—Aunt Evie wouldn't notice if I suddenly started walking around on my ears— but I figured it might help if the unicorns thought there was someone back home who would care if I disappeared.

"Naaaaaay," the unicorn leader replied. Then he lunged forward and jabbed my elbow with his horn.

"Ow!" I cried as pain shot through my entire arm.

The unicorn came at me again, but I ducked out of the way just in time. Instead of spearing me, the unicorn's horn sliced into the trunk of the tree. He whinnied and kicked, trying to get himself unstuck.

Seeing my chance, I jumped to my feet and sprinted away. From behind me came an angry, horselike bellow. I didn't need to speak unicorn to know what it meant.

I could hear the unicorns galloping after me. I tried to run faster, but my arm was throbbing. Were unicorns' horn tips poisonous?

As the sound of hooves grew louder, I realized I wouldn't last much longer. Besides the pain in my arm, my legs were starting to feel like lead. Any second I would run out of steam.

"Anthony," I said, panting. "Wherever you are, please help me."

A split second later, I heard a loud *Pop!* and Anthony the Gnome materialized in front of me. He was grinning from ear to ear and holding a giant ice-cream cone.

"Hey, Jenny-girl. Did you miss me?" he said.

I grabbed Anthony's arm and pulled him along as I ran. "Get us out of here!"

Anthony rolled his eyes like he always did when he thought I was overreacting. But he held up his free hand and snapped his fingers, managing to lick his ice cream and keep running at the same time.

With another *Pop!* I was pulled out of the unicorns' land, tossed around in the void between worlds, and spit back onto my bedroom carpet.

Home.

I rolled over onto my side and moaned in pain. My arm felt like it was melting.

"Looks like I missed all the fun," said Anthony. "But I found the most amazing dairy stand—"

"Help me!" I croaked.

Anthony's grin faded when he saw the blood gushing onto my sleeve. He balanced his ice-cream cone on my desk. Then he reached into the leather pouch around his waist and pulled out a glass jar filled with green goo.

"This should help," he said cheerfully. He opened the jar and slapped some of the goo onto my arm before I could object.

"Ouch!" I said as my arm started to burn. "Ew!" I added as I caught a whiff of rotting seaweed. But a second later the burning stopped and my arm felt a whole lot better.

"You're welcome," said Anthony. He started wrapping a bandage above my elbow, humming a little tune under his breath.

"I'm supposed to thank you? I almost died!"

Anthony let out a deep laugh that made his round belly jiggle. "Always the drama queen. As if those unicorns would actually hurt you."

"They *did* hurt me. Where do you think all that blood came from?"

"Oh," said Anthony, waving his hand. "That's just how they are. It's nothing to worry about."

"That's what you said about the baby dragons last week before they tried to turn my head into a flaming volleyball."

Anthony laughed again and tugged on his orange beard. "They were just playing. No harm done. You can barely see your scar."

I groaned and lay back on my bed. My entire body ached. I couldn't remember the last time I'd gotten a good night's rest. All I wanted was to curl up in bed with a book about an everyday kid with everyday problems and let it soothe me to sleep.

"No time to loaf around, Jenny-girl," Anthony sang. "I just got word from the Committee that there's another adventure you need to go on today."

I nearly choked. "Another one? Anthony, that's the fifth one this week!"

"Everyone keeps requesting to be saved by you, Jenny-girl. You've got quite the reputation."

I wasn't sure what I'd done to earn that reputation. I didn't even really *like* being an adventurer. But somehow I'd gotten stuck doing it practically nonstop for the past three years. If I ever figured out how to go back in time, I'd tell my nine-year-old self to run the other way when a gnome showed up in her room promising a life of magic and adventure.

"There has to be someone else the Committee can send," I said. "What about all the other adventurers out there?" I hadn't actually met any of the others, but Anthony was always reminding me that they'd kill to be sent on as many missions as I was.

"You're the one they want," said Anthony.

I groaned again and tried to sit up, but my body weighed a ton and my arm was still throbbing. "I can't. I'm too tired."

"Have some candy!" Anthony pulled a bag of enormous gummy worms out of his pocket. "These will wake you right up."

"I'm too tired to even chew. I need to get some sleep. If the Committee members can't understand that, then I can go explain it to them myself."

Anthony rolled his eyes. "You know you can't do that. The Committee stays hidden for its own safety."

I rolled my eyes right back. Maybe the Committee stayed in hiding because its members knew otherwise they'd have angry adventurers coming to find them all the time. Just because the mysterious Committee protected the magical worlds didn't mean it could totally take over my life. I mean, hadn't they ever heard of child labor laws?

"I'm serious," I said, jamming a pillow over my head. "I need to sleep."

"The Committee's not going to like this," Anthony's muffled voice answered. For a minute, everything was quiet. I could picture him standing there with his arms crossed, impatiently tapping his foot.

Finally, I heard him sigh and walk over to my desk. I imagined him scooping up his ice-cream cone and giving it a big lick.

"And they say you're the best," Anthony muttered. Then there was a loud *Pop!* and he was gone.

I pulled the pillow off my head and stared at the empty space where Anthony had been. A small puddle of melted ice cream oozed across my math homework.

I tried not to let what Anthony had said bother me, but it was no use. Everyone expected me to be a superhero, but even superheroes had to sleep sometimes, didn't they? Besides, I wasn't really a hero. I just helped out magical creatures once in a while. No capes or masks involved. And in the end, I was still just a regular girl, wasn't I?

Chapter 2

The next morning, I hurried to get ready for school, knowing it was only a matter of time before Anthony popped in and dragged me away on another adventure. Until then, I could pretend to be going about a normal day like anyone else.

When I was dressed, I took my favorite bracelet out of my jewelry box and put it around my wrist. The bracelet had once been my mother's, and I liked to think it was lucky. Its purple gems sparkled back at me like they were smiling. I didn't usually wear the bracelet because I was afraid of losing it, but given how crazy my adventures had been recently, I wanted all the luck I could get.

Since it was still early, I grabbed my mini-golf club and my favorite pink ball from my closet and took a few practice shots. Everyone needs a way to relax, right? The first ball went into the cup without a problem, but then my arm started to ache and my aim went all off. Stupid unicorns. Thanks to Anthony's magical stinky goo, my wound had almost healed, but bending my arm still hurt. I finally gave up on practicing my swing and trudged down the stairs.

"And how are you feeling today?" I heard my aunt ask from the kitchen. I knew the question wasn't aimed at me, but I wished for once it was. "Did you tell your owner you were angry with her?" Aunt Evie added. A chorus of twitters answered.

I peeked into the kitchen. Aunt Evie had a dented clipboard in her hands and a coffee-stained lab coat draped over her shoulders. She was surrounded by a dozen birdcages, each with a parakeet inside.

"Aunt Evie?" I said over the chirps.

"Yes?" My aunt glanced over with her usual look of confusion, like she was trying to figure out if I were some strange new breed of monkey. Aunt Evie was a veterinary psychotherapist, which meant she was good at talking to animals. People, on the other hand, always seemed to puzzle her.

"My arm hurts," I said.

"Aw," Aunt Evie cooed as she scratched the top of my head. "Why don't you drink some tea?" Tea was my aunt's cure for everything. For animals, she had any kind of medicine imaginable, but she seemed to think that all people ever needed was a nice, strong cup of Earl Grey.

"What if my head fell off?" I asked. "Would you still tell me to drink tea?"

"Hmm," Aunt Evie said, giving me a rare smile. "I suppose in that case I would tell you to pour it down your neck hole."

"Good one," I said. The only family trait my aunt and I had both inherited was a weird sense of humor. From what little I remembered about my father, he'd had it too.

Aunt Evie looked back down at her clipboard, and the moment was over. She marked something on a form and chewed on her pencil. Then she poked the pencil in between the bars of a cage so that one of the parakeets could chew on it too.

I guessed that was the end of family bonding time. I stifled a sigh and went to fix myself some cereal. Aunt Evie meant well, but she had no clue how to take care of anything that wasn't covered in fur or feathers.

I knew it was pointless, but every once in a while I couldn't help imagining what my life would've been like if my parents hadn't disappeared when I was little. I could almost see it in my mind, like a movie shot through a fuzzy lens. Since my memories of my parents were pretty vague, I imagined they were beautiful and always smiling, kind of like Ken and Barbie, only less creepy and proportioned like real people.

My parents had actually both been dentists, but I liked to imagine them as movie stars. The three of us would be living in a mansion with a huge swimming pool. I would come down the giant, curved staircase and tell my parents that my arm hurt. They would stop whatever they were doing and rush over to me. My mother would order the head chef to whip up some of his finest hot cocoa, and my father would challenge me to a game of thumb war (which I would promptly win, of course). And then we'd all pile into a limo and go mini-golfing.

Pretty much all of my lovey-dovey-family fantasies ended with me and my parents playing mini-golf with the sun setting in the background. That probably would have sounded dumb to anyone else, but I couldn't think of anything more perfect.

"Okay, Aunt Evie, I'm off to school," I announced when I was done with breakfast.

"Have fun with the other pups," she called, waving her clipboard.

I hurried out of our squawking kitchen and went down the narrow street toward the bus stop. At the end of the road was Dr. Bradley's weathered old house.

As usual, the doctor was out hobbling around in his front yard, poking at things in the yellow grass with his cane.

"Good morning, Jenny!" he called over the rotting wooden fence. His smile was so wide that I could almost see where his dentures ended. "Look what I found today!" He pointed at something that looked like a chewed-up Frisbee.

"One man's junk is another man's treasure!" I said before I could stop myself. Sometimes the cheesy sayings that came out of my mouth during adventures managed to pop out at other times too. But Dr. Bradley didn't seem to mind my fortune-cookie wisdom. In fact, his smile only grew wider.

"I can't wait to find a spot for this on my wall," he said, looking at the mangled piece of red plastic. Since the doctor's house looked abandoned, people were always dumping their trash in his yard. Dr. Bradley didn't seem to mind that his property was mistaken for the town dump. In fact, he loved sifting through all the old typewriters and toaster ovens and finding "pieces with character" to decorate his house with.

All right, so the doctor was pretty strange. But he was also one of the nicest people I'd ever met. And he made the best butterscotch pudding on earth.

"Is that a battle wound I see?" Dr. Bradley asked, coming over to take a look at my bandaged arm. He'd been a doctor in England before he retired, but unlike Aunt Evie, Dr. Bradley seemed to prefer dealing with people. "They smell a little nicer," he always said.

"It's nothing."

"Tell me about this latest mission," Dr. Bradley said, his eyes twinkling behind his round glasses.

When my adventures had first started, Anthony had warned me not to tell anyone about them, not even my friends. I'd been really careful about following the rules, but somehow Dr. Bradley had managed to get the truth out of me, and I'd been sharing my adventures with him ever since. I didn't really think that counted as breaking the rules since Dr. Bradley clearly thought I was just "using my imagination." He didn't seem to notice that I was way too old for that kind of thing.

"I tried to break up a unicorn fight yesterday," I said.

Dr. Bradley raised his bushy eyebrows. "I always thought of unicorns as peaceful creatures."

So had I. But I was never going to make that mistake again. "Apparently they go crazy for rainbows," I said. "A giant one appeared in their field, and they were all fighting over it."

"So what did the brave Jenny the Adventurer do?" Dr. Bradley asked, clearly expecting to hear about my heroic triumph.

"Well, they wouldn't listen to me. I tried to tell them that they needed to learn how to share. You know, all that 'Caring is sharing!' stuff. But I think unicorns' heads are filled with glitter because they turned on me."

"Turned on you?" The doctor's gray eyes widened.

"They started chasing me and stabbing at me with their horns," I said, shivering at the memory. "I probably would have died if Anthony hadn't finally gotten me out of there."

"Ah yes, Anthony the Gnome. How is your colorful guide?"

Annoying. Candy-obsessed. Useless. "Same as usual," I said aloud. "Sometimes I wonder if I'd be better off going on adventures by myself."

"Well, you are very independent," said Dr. Bradley. "But what will happen to Anthony if he's no longer your guide?"

"I'm sure there's a circus somewhere that would take him."

Dr. Bradley let out a deep, purring laugh. "I'm afraid their supply of cotton candy wouldn't stand a chance."

"It would be gone in minutes." I chuckled as I imagined Anthony eating his way out of a vat of cotton candy. Then my arm started throbbing again and the image disappeared. "I've been thinking that maybe I'm not meant to be doing all this adventuring stuff."

"Really?" said the doctor. "But why?"

"It's just not fun anymore." The moment I said it, I realized it was true. When Anthony had first popped into my life three years earlier, he'd told me I was lucky to be chosen so young, and that the Committee believed I would be a natural. He'd also promised that adventuring would be the most fun I'd ever had. At first he'd been right, but now…"I never have time for school. Or friends. A math test sounds more exciting than going to save another magical world."

Dr. Bradley took off his glasses and blew on them until they were foggy. Then he stuck them back on his nose. "I suppose there is a bit of adventure in having a normal life," he said. "But I seem to remember a time when you enjoyed being a hero."

"For a while, I did." After all, I'd gotten to travel to tons of exotic, magical worlds and save the day. Most of the time, I just had to say one of the cheesy things that popped into my head, like "Waste not, want not!" and the magical creatures would think I was wise and great and do whatever I told them.

In fairy tales, elves and fairies all seemed powerful and clever, but I'd found that wasn't true at all. Most of the magical creatures I'd met had a hard time doing the most basic things on their own. They weren't powerless or dumb; they'd just always had people like me to help them. They'd never had to do anything on their own.

"Do you really think you could leave adventuring for good?" Dr. Bradley asked. His glasses were finally unfogged again, so I could see his worried eyes.

"I don't know," I said. "It doesn't really seem worth it anymore."

At the end of my adventures I was usually rewarded with jewels or servants or anything else I wanted, which had also been exciting at first. But there was nowhere left to keep those kinds of presents in Aunt Evie's tiny house. My closet was already stuffed full of treasure chests. The treasure would come in handy when I was older, but who would accept gold coins from a twelve-year-old without asking too many questions? Besides, having fancy gifts wasn't fun unless you could share them with other people. One thing I never got out of my adventures was friends. The creatures I helped went back to their normal lives in their own worlds, and I went back to my abnormal life in mine.

"Well, I have to go to school," I said.

"Stop by anytime!" said Dr. Bradley. "I just made a batch of butterscotch pudding. And I never grow tired of hearing your amazing stories."

I pretended not to notice the concerned look on the doctor's face as I walked away.

Chapter 3

As the bus rolled along on the way to school, I realized it was the first time all week I'd made it this far. Usually Anthony woke me up first thing in the morning and whisked me away before I'd even had time to brush my teeth—nothing like saving the day when you still had morning breath! I couldn't remember the last time I'd spent the entire day at school. Usually Anthony would do some of his magic, and my tests would be passed and my homework completed without me having to actually do anything.

Weird as it was, I actually kind of missed doing my assignments. Even a whole, uninterrupted day at school sounded nice.

Pop!

A mop of flaming hair appeared in the seat in front of me. It was Anthony.

"Are you insane?" I hissed. "You're not supposed to pop up in public."

"The Committee said I had to find you right away," said Anthony, his voice booming through the entire bus. As he turned around, I saw two green frogs perched on his shoulders. They were about twice the size of regular frogs, and each wore a tiny cape around its neck, one red and one blue.

"An elf!" someone screamed from the seat behind me.

"I am *not* an elf," Anthony said.

"Greetings, Jenny the Adventurer," one of the frogs croaked.

"A talking frog!" someone else cried.

"Ahhh!" everyone shrieked as the bus suddenly lurched forward and we went flying off our seats. I looked up to see the bus driver staring into the rearview mirror. His eyes were locked on Anthony and the frogs, his face frozen in terror.

"Help me!" I called to Anthony as I rushed up to the bus driver. I tried waving my hand in front of the driver's face, but it was as if his eyes were made of glass. The bus started to veer off the road.

"Step on the brake!" I yelled. The driver didn't move. I

turned to Anthony. "You need to make this bus stop before we all die!"

Anthony rolled his eyes. "Always such drama with you, Jenny-girl."

"We're in grave danger," the blue-caped frog said while the other frog covered its eyes.

I glared at Anthony. "Do you want to go back and tell the Committee that you killed a busload of humans?"

His face went all pouty, and I knew I'd won. Anthony held up his hand, snapped his fingers, and disappeared. Instantly, the bus driver came out of his trance and got the bus on the road again. The other kids sat in confused silence for a second before going back to talking and laughing as if nothing had happened.

"We're still here, by the way," I heard Anthony's voice say from somewhere beside me.

I groaned as I sunk back down in my seat. "Haven't you caused enough trouble?" I whispered.

"The Committee insisted that—"

"Shh! We can talk in a minute. When we're not in public."

"Fine," Anthony's voice said. I could imagine him sticking his pointy tongue out at me. Why wasn't I allowed to tell anyone about magic, but he could do whatever he wanted? If I ever met the Committee, I would talk myself hoarse listing all the things that didn't seem fair about being an adventurer.

Finally, we pulled up at the school, and I filed off the bus with the other kids. Everyone was acting like the bus ride had been totally normal. A side effect of magic seemed to be that regular people forgot all about it once it was over.

As I got off the bus, two girls with identical backpacks walked by. I tried to tell myself to ignore them. I tried to tell myself that I didn't have to talk to them this time. I tried—

"Hi, Trish. Hi, Melissa," I said, waving. Apparently, I wasn't in the mood to listen to myself.

The girls looked at me and then glanced at each other, just like they had the last time I'd broken down and spoken to them.

"Do we know her?" Trish said in a loud whisper.

"She doesn't look familiar," Melissa answered.

The two girls kept walking, leaving me standing alone on the sidewalk. Trish and Melissa had once been my best friends, but for almost two years they'd been acting like I was a complete stranger. I didn't know what I'd done wrong. One day they'd just stopped talking to me, making it clear they didn't want to be friends with me anymore.

As I watched Trish and Melissa toss their hair over their shoulders in unison, my chest tightened. Maybe if I wasn't an adventuring weirdo, my friends might actually like me again.

"Jenny!" Anthony called from around the side of the building.

I sighed and hurried over to him and the two frogs. "Okay, so what's the problem?"

"Mistress Jenny," said the blue-caped frog, "my name is Crong and this is Ribba."

"Hi!" the frog in the red cape croaked, waving. She had a swirly design painted onto her green arm, almost like a froggy henna tattoo.

"We have been sent from the kingdom of Speak to beg for your help," Crong continued. "Our land has been under the rule of a terrible sorcerer named Klarr for years. Weeks ago, he kidnapped our prince and locked him in a dungeon. Several adventurers have tried to rescue him, but none have succeeded."

"And what makes you think I can help?" I asked.

"The Committee said that, despite your youth, you are the best adventurer there is," said Crong. "If you can't find the prince, then no one can."

"No pressure," Anthony chirped.

I gave him a look. I wanted to tell all three of them to go away and leave me alone. Was it too much to ask to have one quiet day at school? But as the frogs looked up at me with their pleading eyes, I knew I couldn't say no. As annoying as being an adventurer was sometimes, I couldn't just turn my back on creatures that needed my help. "Okay, let's get this over with."

"Yay! You're really going to help us?" Ribba asked, jumping up and down on Anthony's shoulder.

"Doesn't seem like I have much of a choice. If I don't go with you now, you'll just keep scaring everyone at my school."

"It was not our intention to frighten your friends," said Crong.

His words stabbed at me like glittering unicorn horns. I didn't have friends at school, not anymore. But it was better that way, I told myself. My life was busy enough as it was.

"Ready?" croaked Crong. He hopped on my shoulder as Anthony grabbed my elbow.

Pop!

The school blurred into a million specks of light. I

closed my eyes and braced myself. Even after all this time, I still hated every second of traveling in between worlds. It was like being tossed around in a dryer, only without the nice-smelling dryer sheets.

When I could feel solid ground under my feet again, I opened my eyes and glanced around. What the—?

I opened my mouth in surprise, but one of the frogs hopped into it before I could scream.

"We must be quiet, Mistress," Crong whispered in my ear from his perch on my shoulder. That meant the frog in my mouth was Ribba. I tried to push the frog out with my tongue, but Ribba wouldn't budge. She was like a large, slimy cough drop.

I breathed through my nose in bursts, trying to keep from panicking. Spread out across endless rolling fields were hundreds, maybe thousands, of animals. The fact that they were all staring at me was creepy. The fact that none of them had mouths was terrifying.

Chapter 4

As I stood there like a statue, one of the mouthless creatures came toward me. It was a large, woolly sheep with kind eyes. But below her nose, there was just nothing, not even a dent where a mouth should have been. Its not-thereness made me feel a little sick.

The sheep came up and nudged my hand with her nose. Then she nodded and stepped back. I wasn't sure what to do, but I tried to bow my head without swallowing Ribba. The frog shifted uncomfortably in my mouth.

A few other mouthless creatures scurried over to me, among them a squirrel, a lizard, and something that looked like a four-legged, beakless chicken. The animals held out bunches of tulips so yellow that I almost expected them to smell like lemons. I bowed my head again and took the flowers, smiling in spite of myself. I hadn't been greeted like this in a long time. It was nice to be honored instead of attacked.

The creatures lowered their eyes and retreated back into the crowd. I spotted a family of mouthless rabbits nearby, the babies peering up at me like I was some kind of god. Nothing was cuter (and stranger) than a tiny baby bunny with no mouth.

"Now you must wave," Crong said softly in my ear.

I lifted a shaking hand and gave the best screw-in-the-lightbulb wave I could. The sea of eyes watching me seemed to smile in response. The creatures' mouthless faces looked so hopeful. Clearly, they were all counting on me.

The sheep stomped one of her hooves and the crowd turned. When she stomped again, the crowd ran off across the hills, the woolly sheep leading the way. It was amazing to see so many different kinds of animals running together, kind of like watching a zoo marathon.

When the dust settled, my mouth opened and Ribba shot out.

"Phew!" the frog said as she landed on the grass by my feet. "No offense, Jenny, but your mouth is smellier than a patch of stinkweed."

"Um, thanks," I said. Good thing she'd caught me on a day when I'd actually had time to brush my teeth. "I didn't ask you to jump in there."

"Forgive her, Mistress," said Crong, giving Ribba a stern look.

"I had to do it," said Ribba. "You're not allowed to speak while Her Majesty is honoring you."

"What just happened?" I asked. "Who were all of those...creatures?" I looked toward the hills again, but all the animals had disappeared. Other than a sprawling stone wall in the distance, there was nothing to see but blindingly green grass under a bright blue sky. This didn't look like a kingdom that had been taken over by an evil sorcerer. It could have been the setting of an allergy-medicine commercial.

"Those were the citizens of Speak," said Anthony, twisting the end of his beard with his plump fingers. "They came to get a look at you, to see what all the fuss is about."

"Couldn't you have warned me that they were going to be so...mouth challenged?"

"And miss seeing the look of total terror on your face?" Anthony asked with a chuckle. "Where would be the fun in that?"

"It is a great honor to be nosed by the Queen herself," said Crong. "You are the first adventurer she has greeted in this way."

"That sheep was the Queen?" I'd never met royalty that was quite so…fluffy.

"She is called Queen Ewe," Crong went on. "Her son, Prince Lamb, is who you will be rescuing. The queen is one of the greatest leaders our land has ever seen. It's a shame her rule has been marred by Klarr's occupation."

It was rare to hear anyone talk that way about royalty. Usually, creatures couldn't wait to get rid of their kings and queens. If Queen Ewe really was so beloved, it would feel good to help get her son back.

"So how come you guys have mouths?" I asked the frogs.

Crong let out a long sigh, like my question had pained him. "We are among the few who were immune to the Silence spell."

"I was the only one in my whole swamp who could talk," said Ribba.

"Okay, well, my job here is done," Anthony announced. He grabbed the flowers out of my hand. "I can take these since you won't be needing them. They'll be perfect for my sister's birthday tomorrow. She said I'm not allowed to give her any more candy."

"Wait, aren't you going to help?" Why did Anthony

even bother calling himself my guide when he was always running off during my adventures?

Anthony conjured a giant chocolate bar out of thin air. "I was asked to deliver you here, and here you are. So that means I'm done." He unwrapped the end of the candy and took a bite.

"Fine," I said. "But if I call for you, come right away this time, okay?"

Anthony rolled his eyes. "Okay, okay," he said, his mouth still stuffed. "Have fun." He disappeared with a *Pop!* leaving behind the scents of chocolate, caramel, and tulips.

I turned back to the frogs. "So tell me more about this place. Why is it called Speak? Isn't that a little, um, cruel?"

"The history of Speak is long and tragic," Crong said with a graceful wave of his green arm. "There was once a time when it had a different name, just as its citizens were different. But nearly twenty years ago, when Klarr cast his Silence spell over our kingdom, the citizens decided it was time for a change. Their hope is reflected in the name they gave their newly hushed kingdom." Crong hopped forward, his voice suddenly an intense whisper. "And since then they have waited patiently, silently, for someone to save them and to restore their ability to truly *speak* once more."

After a dramatic pause, Ribba started clapping her tiny frog hands. "Bravo!" she said. "You haven't lost any of your talent, Crong!"

The frog grinned, clearly pleased with himself, before giving a little bow.

"Crong used to be a renowned actor before he joined the League," Ribba informed me.

"What league?"

"Over the years, those of us with magical abilities have banded together and made it our mission to restore our kingdom's previous glory," said Crong. "Ribba is the newest addition to our order."

"I can't do much," she said with a modest shrug. "Just a little spell here and there. Before this, I just worked at a salon."

"A salon?" I repeated. "You mean like a place where animals get their fur curled?"

"Of course not!" said Ribba. "Curls are *so* out of style right now. These days everyone wants their fur crimped for that carefree llama look."

Wow. This place just kept getting weirder. "And the League has actually been trying to stand up to this Klarr guy?" I asked.

Crong nodded. "As much as we can. Of course, none of us are adventurers like you."

"But you're magical!" I said. "I can't even make a coin disappear. You all just need to work together." The frogs stared at me. Clearly, in their eyes, an adventurer was a hero, no matter what skills she did or didn't have. "There's no *I* in team!" I tried again. The minute the words were out of my mouth, I groaned. Maybe the Committee had implanted some kind of chip in my brain that made corny sayings pop into my head.

"Actually, we spell things a little differently here," said Crong. "In our kingdom *team* does have an *i*. And a silent *x*."

I shook my head. "Never mind."

Still, I had to admit I was impressed that the creatures had managed to organize themselves into a league at all. In most worlds I'd visited, the inhabitants just used their magic for simple things like boiling water. None of them ever thought to band together and try to take control of their own kingdoms. Instead, they begged for help from the Committee, who then sent Anthony barging into my room practically every day.

"So why does this Klarr guy hate mouths so much?" I asked.

"Everyone thinks it's because the sorcerer was born without a mouth, so the sight of them makes him totally crazy," said Ribba.

"Does that mean no one in Klarr's kingdom has a mouth either?"

"He has allowed some of his servants to keep theirs," Crong said. "It is how he ensures their loyalty. But the rest have been affected just as the creatures of Speak have."

That meant Klarr was the worst kind of bad guy: he'd do anything to anyone, even harming those who were loyal to him. This mission was starting to sound harder and harder.

"Does Klarr control all of Speak?" I asked.

"Yes," said Crong. "His soldiers defeated Queen Ewe's army years ago. But the sorcerer remains in the kingdom of Klarr." He pointed to the stone wall I'd spotted earlier. It stretched all the way across the horizon, dividing Klarr's kingdom from the kingdom of Speak. When I squinted, I could just make out some towers beyond it. They had to be really tall to be visible from so far away.

"Klarr named his own kingdom after himself?" I shook my head in disgust. Why did all bad guys have to be so self-centered? If I had a kingdom, I wouldn't go and name it Jennyland. "You said other adventurers have been sent to find the prince. What happened to them?"

Crong lowered his eyes. "Four of them were sent."

"They all disappeared," Ribba added in an ominous tone.

Hearing that didn't exactly make me feel brave. But there was no point in standing around and psyching myself out. Princes didn't rescue themselves, did they?

"Well, I guess we should get going," I said, aiming my feet at the faraway castle in the kingdom of Klarr. After a moment I realized the frogs weren't following me. "What?"

"Are you suggesting that we *walk*, Mistress?" asked Crong.

"Yeah, why not?"

"I guess we *could* do that," said Ribba, as if it was the last thing on earth—or wherever we were—that she would want to do.

"Okay, then what do you suggest?" I asked, trying not to sound annoyed. *They* had come to *me* for help, after all. Didn't that mean I was in charge?

"We could use our magic to transport us there, Mistress," offered Crong. "Then our journey would be quite swift."

"Oh." Once again I was impressed that these creatures actually knew how to use their magical abilities for something useful. That just proved my point that the kingdom of Speak didn't need my help. They had enough magic to fix their own problems.

The frogs got into position on my shoulders. *Pop!*

This time the journey was much faster. Within seconds, we were a few feet away from a castle so big that I couldn't believe it was real. Even the ivy climbing up the stone walls was prehistorically gigantic. The exterior wall curved away from us in both directions, so the castle seemed to be shaped like a circle. In front of the hulking main door were four huge statues of dancing circus bears.

"This place is enormous!" I said. Then I saw something fly out from behind one of the giant castle towers. "Get down!" I barely had time to scream before we were attacked by the biggest, scariest monster I'd ever seen.

Chapter 5

My hair whipped around my head as the monster flew past. With its shimmering wings and silvery, round body, it looked like a cross between a dragonfly and a submarine.

"Halga, you bewitching ogre!" I heard Crong cry from somewhere nearby.

"What are you doing?" I whispered, realizing both frogs were standing in plain sight. "Get down!"

"No need to fear, Mistress," said Crong. "Halga is an old friend."

The ground shook under us. I looked up to see the beast landing nearby on two elephant-like rear legs. Her head reminded me of a silver ant's, but the center of her back was lined with what looked like dinosaur spikes. As I stared up at her narrow face, I could swear the monster was wearing glittery eye shadow around her buggy eyes.

"Crong, is that you?" the beast asked in a booming voice.

"It is indeed!" said Crong. "Is guarding castles how you're keeping busy these days?"

Halga shrugged her giant, silver shoulders, her wings fluttering behind her. "Not many job openings for washed-up actresses," she said.

I dared to raise my head a little higher as Crong hopped to the beast and gave her giant toe a big hug. "Is it really safe?" I asked Ribba.

Ribba flicked her tongue. "Halga's pretty harmless, even though she could use some serious makeup tips. But Crong can't control himself around her. He's the one you need to keep an eye on."

I watched as Crong tried to tickle Halga's enormous foot. The beast let out a giggle, sending out a gust of wind that made my head snap back. Then Crong waved his froggy legs around and—*poof!*—a sparkling rock appeared.

"It's beautiful!" cried Halga, scooping the rock up with one of her front claws. Her nails were covered with sparkly polish. "And so shiny!"

Ribba hopped onto my shoulder, her green lips pressed together. "They used to be a couple back in their theater days," she said. "But after Crong joined the League, they were always on different sides of the kingdom. He still talks about her *all* the time."

I couldn't stop staring at the couple. It was the weirdest pairing I'd ever seen. One misstep from Halga, and Crong would be crushed.

Then an angry horn sounded nearby, snapping me back to reality. "Crong!" I called.

The frog held up one of his tiny hands as if putting Halga on hold and then hopped to my side. "Yes, Mistress?"

"Now that we're at the castle, how do we get to the dungeon?" Besides the oversized wooden door, there didn't seem to be another way in. I couldn't even see any windows.

"I was just discussing strategy with Halga," he said. "She has no loyalty to Klarr, you may be sure. She will see to it that we get inside safely."

"Good. Then we'd better go now. I don't know what that horn was, and I don't want to find out."

"Halga has informed me there is an entrance nearby that will lead us straight to the dungeon." He pointed in the direction of one of the towers. Now that we were up close, I realized the towers' roofs were covered in red-and-yellow-striped fabric. Klarr certainly had some interesting decorating ideas.

"How many guards will there be in the dungeon?" I asked.

"Most likely dozens," said Crong, "but fear not. With our magic and your, er, adventurousness, we should have no troubles. Halga will guard the entrance from the outside so that we will not be followed." He gazed lovingly at the beast.

"All right. Let's go."

We went around the castle, weaving our way through enormous bushes and trees until finally we came to the dungeon entrance. It was little more than a big hole in the wall with stairs leading down from it. Crong and Ribba hopped in first. Then it was my turn to go through the door.

The stairs seemed to go on forever, and I had to look down the entire time to keep from stumbling on the uneven steps. By the time we finally saw a light below, my neck was aching from being bent at the same angle for so long.

I gave the frogs a signal, and together we burst through the doorway at the bottom of the steps. We found ourselves facing three oversized guinea pigs dressed in shiny armor. I could just imagine how thrilled Aunt Evie would be to meet guinea pigs that stood on their hind legs and were nearly as tall as I was.

The guards scrambled to clap small, flat plates of metal over their furry mouths and secure them in place with rubber bands. Since Klarr hated mouths, I figured the masks were part of the guards' uniforms.

"What are you doing in here?" asked one of the guards, his voice muffled by the metal plate.

"Why do you have mouths?" asked another.

"Have you come to hurt us?" asked the third as he cowered behind the first two.

"To answer your questions," said Crong, "we are here to rescue one of your prisoners. We have mouths because we were unaffected by the Silence. And if you do not let us pass, we *will* be forced to hurt you."

The guards looked terrified for a moment. Then they all let out high-pitched squeals and started trying to scamper away on all four legs. But since they were all running in different directions, they only managed to crash into each other. Then they began to apologize.

"I didn't see you there."

"No, it was my fault."

"Is my nose bleeding?"

The first two guards crowded around the third and peered at his pink nose. They had completely forgotten about us.

I could have watched this circus for hours, but I knew

it was only a matter of time before more guards came. We couldn't count on them all being clueless.

"Crong," I whispered, "can you conjure some rope and tie the guards up?"

The frog seemed uncertain for a moment. Then his green face took on a determined look. He waved his tiny arms around until there was a soft *poof!* and a thick rope appeared in front of him. Carefully, Crong conducted the rope through the air so it flew toward the guinea pigs and circled around them. In a minute, all three were tied tightly together.

"Hey!" one of the guards said, finally realizing what was happening.

"You tricked us," said another.

"Why would you do that?" asked the third.

"Sorry," I said. "We're on a mission."

We went down the stone corridor, leaving the guards' pathetic squeals behind. As we went deeper into the dungeon, it got colder and gloomier. I couldn't imagine the prince, or anyone else, having to live here. A few feet away from the first set of prison cells, I spotted a bunch of keys hanging on the wall.

"Well, that's lucky. Seems they're not too big on security here," I said. "Let's split up."

"But how will you know what the prince looks like?" said Ribba.

"He's a mouthless lamb, right?" I said as I handed out the keys. "I think I'll be okay."

Crong and Ribba headed down one hallway, the keys in their mouths. I ran down another corridor, unlocking door after door. Dozens of startled eyes stared back at me through the bars, most of them belonging to various mouthless animals.

Finally, I came to the end of the hall, but there was no sign of the prince. I backtracked and headed down another hallway. At the end was a mouthless boy around my age. Not having a mouth looked even stranger on a human than it did on an animal.

"It's okay," I told him. "We're getting you out of here."

I was just about to unlock his cell door when a horn sounded from down the hall. I whirled around to see Ribba and Crong hopping toward me. A huge, hooded figure was on their heels.

"Mistress, it's Klarr!" said Crong. He turned and shot a beam of light out of his tiny hand, but the sorcerer waved his meaty arm and the beam hit the wall instead.

"Let's get out of here!" I cried as Crong raced to catch up with Ribba.

The two frogs leaped into the air. I braced myself as they sailed onto my shoulders.

The hooded figure was getting closer and closer. He was massive but surprisingly graceful for his size. The hood fell back, and I caught a glimpse of Klarr's face. I couldn't help it: I screamed.

Until that moment, I'd had no clue that Klarr was a clown. But he wasn't just a clown. He was the most terrifying clown I'd ever seen.

His face was painted white; his eyes were outlined with every color of the rainbow; and his curly wig was blood red. Where his mouth should have been was a set of drawn-on lips. They were grinning.

The floor shook under my feet as Klarr's big red shoes clopped toward me. I couldn't look away from his painted face as he drew closer and closer and closer.

Pop!

I waited to feel myself being pulled out of the world. But instead, the frogs disappeared. And I was left all alone to face Klarr.

The sorcerer came to a stop in front of me and reached out his white-gloved hand. I tried to back up, but I couldn't move. My entire body was frozen.

Klarr twisted his fingers, and I gasped as I felt a horrible churning inside of me. My stomach was being wrung out like wet laundry.

"What do you want?" I cried.

Klarr's painted smile only grew wider.

"Let me go or I'll—" I couldn't think of a single threat. I couldn't even think of something cheesy to say. All I could do was stare into the sorcerer's laughing eyes.

Klarr took one more step toward me. I shrieked in pain as he gave my insides another fierce twist.

"Anthony!" I screamed. "Anthony, help me!"

Pop!

I could have cried with relief as Anthony appeared behind Klarr.

"Hey, circus freak!" he called.

Klarr whipped around and focused his attention on Anthony. The sorcerer was easily three times his size.

"Why so glum?" said Anthony with one of his big belly laughs as the sorcerer charged toward him.

I held my breath, afraid that Anthony didn't stand a chance. But suddenly, Klarr froze and grabbed his head as if he was in pain.

Anthony's face lit up. "I know what you need!" He

held up his hand and snapped his fingers. A flood of circus peanuts rained down from the ceiling, covering Klarr in a mound of orange.

Anthony trotted over to me. The minute he touched my shoulder, the pain disappeared and I could move again.

"Let's go!" I said. The pile of circus peanuts wouldn't hold Klarr for long.

"Agreed, Jenny-girl."

I grabbed on to Anthony's arm just as one of Klarr's giant hands emerged from the circus peanuts. A beam of rainbow-colored light burst from his fingertips and fired straight at me.

Pop!

I was ripped out of one world, twisted around, and tossed into another. It took me a second to realize the cold, hard surface under me was my kitchen floor.

"Well, that wasn't so hard," said Anthony.

"Speak for yourself," I shot back. Or at least that's what I would have said if I'd still had a mouth.

Chapter 6

"Oh my," said Anthony as he helped me off the kitchen floor. "To be honest, Jenny-girl, that's not a good look for you."

My fingers flew to my face, feeling the horrifyingly smooth spot where my mouth should have been. I grabbed a spoon off the kitchen table and held it up with a shaking hand. An upside-down, mouthless face stared back at me.

I wanted to scream, but I couldn't—I couldn't make any sound at all! I turned back to Anthony and threw the spoon on the floor.

"What's the matter?" he said.

I couldn't believe it. Was he not seeing what I was seeing? I pointed at my mouth, or lack thereof.

Anthony studied me, his orange eyebrows crinkling. "Do you mean your mouth?" he said finally.

I jumped up and down, as if we were playing the worst game of charades ever.

"Didn't I warn you that might happen?" he said as a box of chocolate-covered raisins appeared in his hands.

I shook my head. I would have remembered a conversation about the possibility of my mouth disappearing.

"Huh," said Anthony, popping some candy in his mouth. "I could have sworn I went over the risks with you before we left for your adventure."

My patience had run out. I stomped over to Anthony and snatched the box of raisins out of his hand. Then I tossed it across the room, where it hit the wall and landed on the floor.

"Hey!" said Anthony. "I was eating those."

The hurt look on his face just made me angrier. Did he really not care that my mouth was gone? Was candy all he ever thought about?

I grabbed my aunt's clipboard from the kitchen table and started scrawling furiously. "Fix this!" I wrote.

"I would if I could, Jenny-girl," said Anthony. "But that would take magic that's way beyond me."

"What am I supposed to do?" I wrote.

Before Anthony could answer, Aunt Evie appeared in

the doorway. She gasped at the sight of a gnome standing in the middle of her kitchen. Then she gasped again when she saw me.

"Oh my." Aunt Evie blinked a few times, her face growing pale. "Would anyone like some tea?" she asked. Then she wandered over to the stove and picked up the teapot, whistling to herself as if we weren't even there.

I turned to Anthony and pointed at the clipboard again.

"We don't have time to think about your mouth right now," said Anthony. "You need to go back and complete your mission."

I couldn't believe it. He had to be joking.

"Don't look at me like that," said Anthony. "Your job was to rescue the prince, and you didn't deliver. The Committee will be far from thrilled."

I didn't care what the Committee thought. "I'm not going anywhere until I get my mouth back!" I scrawled on the clipboard.

Anthony threw up his pudgy hands. "Why do you have to make everything so difficult? None of my other adventurers ever gave me so much trouble."

I held up the clipboard and pointed to the words I'd written before. "Fix this!" The words swam together as my eyes started filling with stupid tears. I wasn't a crier. I'd never been a crier. But even I had my limits.

"How many times do I have to say it, Jenny-girl? There's nothing I can do!"

The annoyed tone in Anthony's voice only made things worse. I didn't think I could hold my tears in a minute longer. The last thing I wanted was for Anthony to tell me I was being a baby.

It was a low blow, I knew, but there was one sure-fire way to get rid of a gnome. I gripped the pen again and wrote in big, angry letters: "Leave me alone, you big, fat ELF!"

Anthony sucked in his breath as he read the words. Then his normally pink cheeks flushed blood red and his nose turned purple. "How *dare* you?"

I turned my face away as a pesky tear rolled down my cheek. I just wanted to be left alone.

"Fine," Anthony spat. "That's what I get for rescuing you." With an ear-splitting *POP!* he was gone.

A moment later, Aunt Evie came up to me with a steaming cup of hot water. She took another look at my mouthless face and went pale all over again. "Oh my," she said. "I forgot to put in a tea bag." She turned and hurried into the pantry.

I had to get it together. Crying was not only pointless but also really hard without a mouth. The stuffier my nose got, the tougher it was to breathe. I wiped my eyes with the back of my hand. There had to be some way to fix this.

Aunt Evie emerged from the pantry, her mug now loaded with a dozen tea bags. She sat down at the kitchen table, still looking shaken.

At that moment the doorbell rang. I was perfectly happy to ignore whoever was at the door until I heard Dr. Bradley call out: "Jenny, are you there?"

The familiar sound of his voice made me feel a little better. He was a doctor, after all. Maybe he could do something to help.

I opened the door a crack, expecting Dr. Bradley to be grinning back at me as usual. But his face was more serious than I'd ever seen it.

"Oh dear," he said. "I was afraid something like this might happen. I think it's best if you come with me."

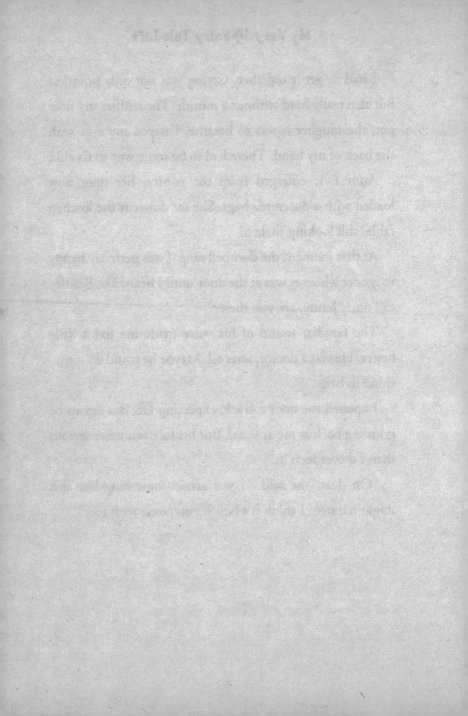

Chapter 7

When I was safely inside Dr. Bradley's house, he led me up the stairs and down a hallway I'd never been in before. He opened a large wooden door, revealing an enormous library. Unlike the rest of the doctor's house, the library was clean and organized and totally junk-free.

If I'd still had a mouth, I would've gasped at the glowing object in the center of the room.

It was an enormous screen with my face plastered right in the middle of it. I watched myself blinking back at myself. It was disorienting. Around the main picture of my face were a few other images: Aunt Evie sipping her tea; Ribba and Crong hopping through a swamp; and Anthony stuffing his face with jelly beans.

The screen wasn't a TV or a monitor. It looked like a thin sheet of water with a reflection on it, almost like a vertical puddle. It hung in midair without wires or hooks or any other logical explanation. If I hadn't spent the past three years around magic, I would have tried to explain the hanging puddle some other way. But I knew magic when I saw it, and clearly Dr. Bradley was the one using it.

What was going on?

"Do not be alarmed, Jenny," said Dr. Bradley. "I know this comes as somewhat of a shock, and I probably should have told you sooner."

He adjusted his bow tie and motioned for me to sit. I made my way over to an antique couch, barely able to feel my legs under me. Dr. Bradley hobbled to a facing armchair and sat down, leaning his cane beside him. A wooden owl was perched on the shelf above the doctor's head, its hollow eyes staring at me like it had never seen a mouthless girl before.

"You see, Jenny, you have done a wonderful job with all of the adventures you were sent on, so there was no need for me to reveal my true identity to you. But now that you have been affected by the Silence spell, it's time you learned the truth. My name really is Dr. Bradley, although I am a doctor of magic, not of medicine. I was an adventurer for many years before I retired and turned to the study of magic."

No way. The doctor had once been an adventurer? I'd wondered what other adventurers might be like and had hoped to meet some my own age one day. But I'd always imagined they'd be more like Indiana Jones than like Dr. Bradley.

"I was hired by the Committee to ensure your safety. You are very important to them." Dr. Bradley adjusted his glasses. "And you are very important to me, Jenny. So I ask that you please not be angry with me for not telling you this sooner."

I didn't know what to think. Dr. Bradley had always been the nice old man down the street who never ran out of butterscotch pudding. But now that I thought about it, there were other odd things about Dr. Bradley besides his obsession with collecting junk. He almost never left his property, and he'd once admitted that I was his only visitor. None of the neighbors believed me when I told them someone lived in the doctor's big old house.

I sighed through my nose. I'd always liked and trusted Dr. Bradley. The fact that he was magical shouldn't change that. He'd always helped me, and he seemed to want to help me now. I wished I could tell the doctor all this, but I had to make do with a few blinks and a nod.

"I am glad you understand," said Dr. Bradley. "Now, I am sure you are eager to get your features back to normal."

I nodded again. That was a serious understatement.

"All right." Dr. Bradley stood and limped over to one of the towering bookshelves. I eyed the books in awe. They looked ancient and mysterious, with titles in languages I didn't recognize. Some of the books had a strange glow around them. Dr. Bradley scanned a few of the books and then pulled one of the glowing ones off the shelf.

"Here we are," he said. "You may want to close your eyes for a moment. It can be a bit bright at first."

I shook my head and kept my eyes open. Whatever was going to happen, I wanted to see it.

Dr. Bradley cracked open the book. It flew out of his hands and landed on the floor. A blinding beam shot out of it, forming a column of colorful light. I squinted until the light dimmed and the colors started to turn into a hologram. It showed an ornate, carved door.

"You see, Jenny," said Dr. Bradley, "some books can transport you to other worlds."

I wished I could groan out loud, but I had to be satisfied with doing it internally. Books as doorways to other worlds? That was one of the cheesiest clichés I'd heard in my adventures. Was the Committee really just a bunch of teachers in disguise? The thought made me cringe.

"The door you see leads into the Committee's waiting room," said Dr. Bradley.

I sat up. Was I finally going to meet the mysterious Committee?

"Ordinarily the Committee stays hidden," the doctor continued. "But when I saw what had happened, I sent a request on your behalf and asked the Committee members to help restore your mouth. They are the only ones with strong enough magic to do so."

I blinked my thanks. Then I pointed at the doctor, but he shook his head.

"I am afraid I cannot go with you," he said. "Only the person with a request for the Committee can go through the portal. Once you enter the waiting room, you will be in a magically protected area, and I will no longer be able to see you on my screen." Dr. Bradley reached into his pocket and took out a cell phone the size of a house cat.

"Here, take my phone with you. But make sure to turn off the ringer. The Committee has very particular rules about that sort of thing. To this day, they haven't forgiven me for the time an alarm went off on my wristwatch. I've had to send a messenger to fetch my paychecks for the past ten years."

I shook my head to try to object. How was I supposed to use a phone when I had no mouth?

"You won't need to call anyone," said Dr. Bradley, as if reading my mind. "After you have spoken with the Committee, the phone will allow me to locate you and bring you home."

I took the phone from Dr. Bradley—it weighed more than an extra large jar of peanut butter—and studied the different buttons until I found one that looked like the volume control. When I'd turned off the sound, I managed to jam the clunky phone in my pocket.

"I suppose that's all," said the doctor. "Once you return, we can sit down and have a nice bowl of pudding."

I realized, suddenly, that it had been hours since I'd eaten. I didn't feel hungry yet, but how long could I go mouthless before I starved to death? I turned to Dr. Bradley and made a few spooning-something-into-my-mouth gestures (or, at least, into where my mouth *should* have been).

"As long as you are under the Silence spell, the magic will keep you from having to eat," said Dr. Bradley. "But once your mouth returns, you will have a healthy appetite. I'll make sure to have some nice prunes waiting for you."

I tried not to crinkle my nose in disgust.

"Then we can figure out a way to get rid of that foul Klarr," Dr. Bradley added.

My disgust was replaced with clawing panic. I had faced a lot of scary bad guys in my adventures, like the Yelling Yeti and the Three-Headed Caterpillar. But none had been as frightening as Klarr; none had made me feel so helpless.

I shook my head until my ears were about to fall off.

Dr. Bradley studied me for a moment. "Do you mean that you won't help defeat Klarr?"

I nodded.

"But the Committee is convinced you are the one for the task, and I must agree. You, my dear, are the most skilled adventurer we have seen in years. Only the most promising begin as young as you did. We chose you because you have great natural talent. That is why you will succeed where the others have failed."

I rolled my eyes. Clearly, I wasn't as good as everyone said if Klarr could take my mouth away with a wave of his finger. Besides, why would I want to go running back to face him when he'd made four other adventurers vanish into thin air? The memory of Klarr's laughing eyes flashed through my mind. The sorcerer had already paralyzed and silenced me; what other terrible things would he do if I had to face him a second time?

"You know you can't simply abandon an adventure," said Dr. Bradley. "The rules say you must see it through until the end."

I didn't care about the rules. I was never going anywhere near Klarr again.

"Look at what that sorcerer has done to you and to thousands of other innocent souls! Will you really let that continue?"

I looked away. Maybe it was selfish, but for once I didn't want to be the one solving problems. Let someone else defeat Klarr. The League seemed capable of handling the situation on its own.

Dr. Bradley's usually bright eyes looked worried. "I had hoped I could count on you for this, Jenny. But it is your decision and I will respect it." He cleared his throat. "Good luck," he said as he escorted me to the portal.

I tried to take a deep breath through my still-stuffy nose. Then I gave Dr. Bradley a parting nod and walked toward the doorway that led into another world.

Chapter 8

When I opened the heavy door, the first thing I noticed was silence. It was the quietest place I'd ever been. Nothing moved, not even the air.

I was in a large waiting room with blindingly white walls and hard metal chairs. Everything smelled crisp and clean, like it had just been scrubbed with soap. I shuffled over to one of the chairs and sat down. On the opposite side of the room was another door, identical to the one I'd just come through. I was tempted to go peek to see where it led, but I didn't want to get caught up in any more trouble. Instead, I tried not to think about my mouth being gone, which meant that was *all* I could think about.

After a long time of sitting in absolute silence, I jumped as the second door opened with a drawn-out creak. I expected to see someone standing on the other side, but no one was there. I hesitated for a moment and then went toward it. The moment I stepped through, the door shut behind me.

I was in an enormous hallway made entirely of white tile. It went on and on, almost like an optical illusion. I could just make out a teeny, tiny something at the end. My footsteps echoed on top of each other as I walked and walked and walked.

Finally, I spotted a long table at the very end of the hall. At it sat four figures, all with the same gray hair, the same round faces, and the same beige sweaters. When I could almost see their faces, a loud voice called out, "Halt, please."

I stopped and stood like a statue.

"Now please walk toward the red circle."

I scanned the floor until I spotted a painted red circle off to the right. I went over and stood in it.

"Exactly in the center, please," the voice said.

Um, okay. I moved over until I was smack-dab in the middle of the circle.

"Now count to ten and proceed to the yellow circle."

I tried to open my mouth to count, but of course that wouldn't work. I settled for counting in my head. Then I went toward the yellow circle, off to the left, and stood perfectly in the center.

"Now count to ten and proceed to the green circle."

Seriously? What was the point of all of this? Then I remembered what Dr. Bradley had said about the Committee having very particular rules. I didn't want to make the Committee members mad before I got my mouth back.

When I was standing in the exact center of the green circle, I studied the four figures seated in front of me. I'd been right in thinking they looked alike. In fact, it was as if someone had taken a plump, middle-aged woman with blue-gray hair and made three exact copies of her.

"Welcome, Jennifer." I couldn't tell if only one of the women had spoken or if all four had. They all moved their mouths at the exact same time, but it only sounded like the voice of one person.

I wanted to explain to them that no one called me by my full name. But, of course, I couldn't say much of anything.

"We are the Committee," the women said. "Dr. Bradley sent you to us to reverse the effects of the Silence."

I nodded.

"We are the only ones with the kind of magic required to undo the effects."

Apparently, the Committee liked to state the obvious.

"Unfortunately, we cannot do so at this time."

Wait, what?

"The paperwork has yet to go through." The women all shook their heads in unison. "Once the appropriate papers have been stamped and signed, we will be able to reverse the spell." The women reached out and simultaneously rang four bells. "Next, please!" they called. Then they looked at me like they expected me to move along.

No way. I crossed my arms in front of my chest. I'd come to get my mouth back, and I wasn't going anywhere until that happened.

The Committee looked at me, clearly confused. "We are finished here now."

I shook my head and stood my ground.

"There is nothing we can do to help you. You must have the proper paperwork. There is no paperwork. Without paperwork, we cannot do anything."

Rage bubbled up inside me like melted cheese. After all the missions I'd been sent on, after all the cuts and bruises, the Committee was refusing to help me because something wasn't *stamped*?

I was about to lose it when a horrible, ear-piercing noise rang out. It sounded like a pack of wolves singing a love song. The Committee members gave me scalding glares while I tried to figure out where the howling was coming from. Then I realized it was the cell phone Dr. Bradley had given me. Oops. Apparently, I hadn't turned the sound off after all.

I tugged at the hulking phone, but it was much harder to get out of my pocket than in. I pulled and pulled until finally it flew out and landed on the floor. The caller ID flashed "Mum" for a second before the phone went silent.

"Unacceptable!" the Committee shouted. "Unacceptable!"

Before I could do anything, invisible hands pulled me into the air and dragged me back the way I'd come. No, I couldn't go yet. Not until I had my mouth back! I struggled to get free, but whatever was holding me was incredibly strong.

I was pulled back through the door and dumped onto the floor of the waiting room. Then everything was still. I jumped to my feet and tried to open the door, but it wouldn't budge. I banged and pounded with my fists, but there was no answer.

Exhausted, I sunk down into one of the chairs. I had officially won the Worst Day of the Year award.

A moment later, I heard the door open on the opposite side of the room. I perked up, thinking Dr. Bradley had come for me. But it wasn't the doctor.

It was Klarr.

For a second, I just sat there, totally frozen. I had to be seeing things. There was no way the clown could have found me here. But when one of his red shoes let out a violent squeak, I snapped back to reality.

I ran to the door that led to the Committee, but it still wouldn't open. I spun around and let out a silent shriek. Klarr was inches away from me. His painted-on mouth was grinning like I was his new favorite toy.

The door on the other side. If I could just make it over there, I might be able to get away.

I tore through the room, circling around Klarr. But just as I was about to reach the other door, a bolt of rainbow-colored lightning flew out of the clown's fingers. It struck my side and pinned me against the wall.

The energy stabbed at me like a million needles. Tears dripped from my eyes. *Please, someone help me*, I thought. *Please.*

Klarr came toward me, his red hair bouncing up and down with each step. His painted smile stretched across his face. *Leave me alone, you creepy clown!* my thoughts shrieked at him. But his eyes just laughed back at me as he came closer and closer and closer...

Chapter 9

When I opened my eyes, it took me a minute to remember what had happened. Then it all came rushing back: the frogs, the Silence, and Klarr's face just inches from mine. I must have passed out.

I sat up and realized I was alone in a dim prison cell. There was no sign of the sorcerer. For now, at least, I was safe. Dr. Bradley was probably coming to rescue me at that very moment. Wait, except that after I'd gone through the portal, he hadn't been able to see me on his big puddle screen, which meant that he had no idea where I was. How had Klarr found me there if the Committee's location was supposed to be secret?

I was in the same dungeon I had tried to rescue Prince Lamb from earlier that day, I realized. Or had it been yesterday? The dungeon was so gloomy that it was hard to tell if it was day or night.

Most of the cells were empty, which meant the prisoners we'd released had managed to get away, but in the cell across from mine was the mouthless boy I'd seen earlier. He was about my age with blond, almost white, curly hair and very pale skin. He looked like he'd never been out in the sun in his life. His round brown eyes glanced over at me, and he held up his hand in a wave.

I gave a weak wave back.

Hello, a voice said.

I froze.

Don't be afraid. It's only me.

The boy from the other cell waved again, but I was convinced the voice hadn't come from him. It sounded more like it had actually been in my head.

If you try to speak with your mind, I should be able to hear you, the voice said.

I tried to form a coherent thought. *Is this thing on?*

Yes! came the reply. The boy waved one more time.

How are you doing this? I asked.

It's called mind-speaking. It's a skill the creatures of my land developed in secret after Klarr cast his spell on us. I suppose it's our own small form of rebellion.

I'm Jenny.

Welcome to the dungeon, Jenny. I'm Prince Lamb.

I jumped off the bunk and ran to the prison bars. *You're Prince Lamb? But you're supposed to be a sheep!*

The boy nodded sadly. *Klarr changed me from my sheep form into this.*

But why?

Because it's better for his act.

His act? I repeated.

I guess humans have better acrobatic skills, said the prince. *My mother will be devastated. She won't want her son to be a freak.* The prince glanced up at me. *No offense.*

I probably should have been miffed at being called a freak, but all I cared about was getting out of the dungeon. I tested the metal bars of the cell, but each one felt solid, as did the lock on the door. There was a tiny window by the ceiling, but there were thick bars across it too.

I recognize you, said Prince Lamb. *You were here earlier with the two frogs. I saw Klarr attack you and take away your mouth.*

We were trying to rescue you. Now Klarr is probably going to kill me.

If he was going to kill you, he would have done it already, said the prince. *He probably only wants to torture you.*

Oh, what a relief!

It's not so bad, Prince Lamb replied. Then his face darkened. *Except when he makes us walk the tightrope. And the trapeze gives me nightmares for days.*

Don't worry, I said. *I'll find a way to get us out of here.*

Our conversation was interrupted by the clanging of approaching armor. Three guards came into view, and I could have laughed as I recognized their guinea-pig faces. If they were all that stood between me and freedom, things were not as bad as they seemed.

The guards stopped in front of my cell and studied me for a moment.

"We know you," said one.

"You tricked us," said another.

"Where did your mouth go?" asked the third.

"She must be the one the sorcerer brought in," said the first. The other two nodded in agreement.

"He does like putting humans in his act," said the second.

"Shouldn't he be here by now?" asked the third.

The last guard's words sent me into panic mode. Klarr was on his way here! I had to find a way out *now*!

There had to be some way to get past the guards. I looked them over and caught sight of the keys dangling at their waists. If I could distract them and get my hands on one of those sets of keys…

I glanced across the corridor and sent Prince Lamb a message: *I have a plan. Pretend to be really sick.*

The prince looked uncertain for a moment. Then he threw himself onto the ground and started writhing in fake pain. I pointed frantically to get the guards' attentions.

"Something is wrong," said one of the guards. I was impressed at how real Prince Lamb's act looked.

"He seems to be in bad shape," said the second.

"What's the matter?" asked the third, kneeling beside the prince.

Then I realized the flaw in my plan. The guards were so concerned about Prince Lamb that they were huddled around him, which meant they were even farther away from me than before.

Act even worse, I told the prince. *Try to scare them.*

Prince Lamb crawled toward the edge of his cell. Then he started throwing himself against the bars, as if he were trying to break them down.

"Stop!" said one of the guards.

"You'll hurt yourself," said another.

"Help?" whimpered the third guard as he backed away.

He drew closer and closer to my cell until he was right in front of me. Carefully, I reached out and wrapped my fingers around the keys. Then I lifted them off the guard's belt and quickly hid them behind my back.

You can stop now, I told the prince.

Prince Lamb's frantic movements ended. He fell onto the ground and lay still.

"Look," said the first guard.

"He seems better," said the second.

"Do you think it's contagious?" asked the third, his voice shaking.

The guards looked at each other and quickly scampered down the hallway. I wanted to laugh as I held the keys up for Prince Lamb to see. His eyes lit up.

Let's get out of here, he said.

As quietly as I could, I unlocked my cell door and crept over to unlock Prince Lamb's. Finally free, we trotted down the hallway, on the lookout for any danger. When we got to the end of the corridor, we spotted the three guinea-pig guards furiously eating heads of lettuce, their ears shaking. I had never seen creatures shoveling food into their mouths so fast.

They eat when they're nervous, the prince told me. *They probably won't even notice we're here.*

We tiptoed around the guards as the sounds of crunching and munching continued. We were almost at the stairs that led out of the dungeon when a loud horn sounded outside.

"Stop them!" one of the guinea pigs cried.

The prince and I scrambled up the stairs as fast as we could, the guards right behind us. When we finally got out into the daylight, we darted around the circle of dancing bear statues. I glanced over my shoulder. The guards were still following, but their short legs weren't carrying them fast enough.

We just have to get into the woods, I said.

We ran even faster until we were among the thick trees. The prince and I wove around branches, under vines, and over rocks. Finally, after we'd waded through a stream, the woods around us were quiet. I pulled Prince Lamb behind a giant tree stump and listened.

I think we lost them, I said, trying to ignore the squishiness of my wet shoes. *Now what do we do?*

Prince Lamb breathed hard through his nose. *We must return to my kingdom.*

Are you sure you want to do that? Klarr will probably send soldiers there to look for you.

My mother needs to know I'm all right. After that, I'll go into hiding.

I shrugged. My mission was to rescue the prince. If he wanted to get himself kidnapped again, that was his business.

We continued on our way, stopping every few minutes to make sure no one was following us. We'd been lucky to lose the guards so easily.

A long while later, when my legs were turning into jelly and my wet feet were starting to feel moldy, we came out into a clearing. I could still make out the giant towers of Klarr's castle over the treetops.

Can we rest for a moment? said Prince Lamb. *Traveling on two legs is much more tiring than traveling on four.*

We're still too close to Klarr's castle, I said. *We need to keep moving.*

Prince Lamb nodded, but I could see how exhausted he was. I glanced up at the castle again and caught sight of something large with glimmering wings sailing through the sky above us.

It was Halga!

I waved my hands in the air to get the monster's attention, but Halga was too high up to notice. Then I remembered my bracelet. I took it off and dangled it in the air, gently moving it back and forth to make the purple gems catch the light.

After a minute, something like a squeal came from the sky, and Halga rushed at the string of sparkling stones. When the monster was within inches of the bracelet, I pulled it behind my back.

Halga came to a screeching halt directly in front of me. "Give me the shiny thing!" she roared.

I shook my head and hoped I wasn't making a big mistake.

Halga stomped over to me. "Who do you think you are, denying me anything?" Then she sat back, puzzled. "You look familiar but different."

I nodded encouragingly and tried to mime a frog-like creature with my free hand.

"You're that girl!" said Halga. "The one that came with Crong!"

I jumped up and down, caught in yet another bad game of charades.

"But what are you doing here? And with no mouth? And who is this boy?"

Since I couldn't explain the situation, I put my hands together in a pleading motion.

"You need a favor?" said Halga.

I nodded. Then I pointed in the direction of Queen Ewe's kingdom and mimed flying.

"If anyone sees me helping you, Klarr will punish me for sure," said Halga. "I already let you into the dungeon, and that was only because Crong asked me to. I can't risk it again."

I put on my best puppy-dog face, but Halga shook her giant head. "I don't think so, adventurer girl."

The sound of a clown horn echoed in the woods. We were running out of time. Klarr was out there somewhere, looking for us. There was no way I was going to let that crazy clown catch me again.

Reluctantly, I held up the bracelet and tried to make it clear that if Halga helped us, the bracelet would be her reward.

The monster's eyes lit up. "Would you really give it to me?"

I nodded, trying to ignore the sinking feeling in my stomach. What did it matter if I had my mother's bracelet if I wasn't alive to appreciate it?

"It's very shiny," said Halga. "All right. I'll help you."

I ran my fingers over the purple stones one more time. Then I forced myself to toss the bracelet at the monster.

Halga caught it easily in her teeth. Then she crouched down and began to lovingly admire her new treasure.

But there wasn't time to waste. The prince clapped his hands, reminding us we had to go.

"All right, all right," said Halga. She clutched the bracelet with one of her claws and then bent her giant head so that we could climb onto her back.

I jumped on and grabbed hold of one of the monster's spikes. Prince Lamb got on behind me. A moment later, Halga shot off the ground and thundered into the sky.

Only when we were high in the clouds did my lungs seem to start working again. I looked down at Klarr's castle and realized that from overhead it didn't look like a castle at all. In fact, its rounded shape and colorful stripes were just like those of a circus tent. Of course.

"Bet you're relieved to be away from there," said Halga over her shoulder.

Relieved wasn't the word. I could have kissed Halga's buggy face for helping us escape.

I scanned the horizon until I caught sight of the queen's palace far off in the distance in the kingdom of Speak. Then I tapped Halga on the shoulder and pointed toward it.

"Next stop, Ewe Central!" she said as she dove so

sharply that my stomach started to protest. I glanced over my shoulder and saw that Prince Lamb's face was turning green. I didn't want to think about what would happen to throw-up if it didn't have a mouth to come out of.

The thought made me feel even woozier, so I tried to focus on the countryside below to steady myself. As I peered at the rolling hills and scattered lakes, I realized that Klarr's kingdom looked a lot like a sprawling mini-golf course.

And how did you win at mini-golf? By getting the ball in the clown's mouth. Too bad this evil clown didn't have one of those.

Finally, we were above Queen Ewe's palace. It wasn't as huge as Klarr's castle, but it was much more inviting. There were white stone towers with bright blue roofs, and stained-glass windows overlooking large white balconies. Come to think of it, it looked exactly like the palace at Disney World. Maybe all those talking Disney animals were actually from the land of Speak.

Where should we land? I asked Prince Lamb.

It's best if we stay out of sight, in case Klarr has spies in the palace. He thought for a moment. *Have Halga land below that window. It's near my mother's private chamber.*

The minute we landed, I tumbled off of the monster's

80

back, glad to be on stable ground again. When my stomach finally calmed down, I turned to Halga and gave her a warm pat on the foot. Prince Lamb gave her a regal bow.

"You're welcome," said Halga, flapping her shining wings. "Now if you could do me one small favor, adventurer girl."

Halga held out a front claw so that I could put on the sparkling bracelet. I just barely managed to latch it around her littlest toe. The sight of it made Halga ooh and ah with joy.

"Best reward I ever got," she said.

Even though it hurt to give the bracelet away, I still wished I could smile. The bracelet had made the monster extremely happy, and Halga had held up her end of the bargain.

"Good luck," she said, giving us a small wave. Then she fluttered into the sky.

Prince Lamb boosted me up so I could push open the window. I took a deep breath and crawled through into the shadows.

Chapter 10

After I'd lowered myself onto the floor of a dark hallway, I turned and helped Prince Lamb climb through the window. The corridor was lined with unlit lamps, and thick tapestries covered the stone walls. Everything looked old and dusty, like no one had bothered to clean it in a long time. This had to be Klarr's doing. He probably wanted Queen Ewe's home to be as dark and depressing as his own.

Prince Lamb led the way as we hurried through one corridor and turned down another. Finally, we came to a doorway where two ferrets stood guard. They wore red sashes with pictures of the queen's face on them and held small but sharp spears. I was surprised to see that they both had mouths.

The moment the guards spotted us, they raised their weapons. They clearly didn't recognize the prince in his non-sheep state.

"Who are you?" one of the guards demanded.

Prince Lamb stepped forward and did a few intricate hand gestures that I couldn't understand. The ferrets peered back at him with suspicion.

"How do we know you're really the prince?" the other guard asked.

Again, the prince did more of the complicated signals. The guards' faces turned from suspicious to overjoyed. They fell to their knees and bowed their heads.

Prince Lamb motioned for them to stand and pointed at the door. The guards stepped aside, and I followed the prince as he went through.

What were all those hand gestures? I asked as we passed through one chamber after another. The rooms were all lavish but run-down and faded, just like the tapestries in the corridors.

The few citizens in my kingdom who still have mouths are unable to mind-speak, said Prince Lamb. *So we have come up with another system of communication.*

Sign language. That makes sense.

You have something like this too? said Prince Lamb.

Yes, I said. *But there aren't too many animals that can do it. Monkeys, mostly.*

Prince Lamb furrowed his brow. Maybe they didn't have monkeys in Speak. But there was no time to explain as we entered the final chamber.

Queen Ewe was reclined on a slab of tarnished gold. When she caught sight of us, she jumped to her four feet, ready to fight. Clearly, she thought we were intruders. But when the queen's gaze fell on me, her face changed. She looked back and forth between me and the prince, obviously confused.

Mother, I heard Prince Lamb say. *It's me.*

The queen's eyes went wide. *Lamb? Can it really be you?*

Yes. Klarr transformed me and trapped me in his dungeon. But Jenny helped me escape.

The queen still looked uncertain, clearly suspecting a trap. She went over to the prince and sniffed him. Finally, she stepped back and shook her woolly head in disbelief. *It is you!* She bent her neck and nuzzled Prince Lamb's hand with her nose. Then she turned to me. *You will be handsomely reward for returning my son to me.*

I felt myself blush. *Oh, that's okay. If you can just figure out a way to send me home, that should be fine.*

The queen's dark eyes widened. *But what about defeating Klarr?*

I thought you were going to help us, said Prince Lamb.

I was asked to rescue you, and I did. I didn't spend all that time running away from Klarr so I could go running back to him.

But our kingdom needs you, said the queen.

I felt bad leaving Speak in Klarr's monstrous hands, but there was no way I'd go anywhere near him again. *I'm sorry, Your Majesty. You'll have to find someone else.*

But Jenny, said the prince, *right before Klarr took away your mouth, there was a moment when he showed weakness. Didn't you see it?*

I thought back to those terrible minutes before Klarr cast the Silence spell on me. The sorcerer had had me paralyzed by his energy beam, and then Anthony had appeared. As I thought about it again, I remembered how Klarr had suddenly grabbed his head as if he'd been in pain. I'd been in so much pain myself that I'd barely noticed it.

He did flinch, I said. *But I don't know what caused it.*

Don't you see? That means there's hope. There might be a way to defeat him. You can't give up now.

I shook my head. I couldn't face Klarr again, not when I hadn't even recovered from his attack. Who knew when

I'd be able to get my mouth back? But I had to admit it was more than that. I was scared, plain and simple. Klarr was more terrifying than any other bad guy I'd gone up against. I knew running away made me a bad adventurer, not to mention a total wimp, but I didn't care. I'd rather be a living coward than a dead hero.

I'm sorry, I said again. *You'll have to ask the Committee to send someone else.*

Queen Ewe's eyes got even wider. Images of stampeding unicorns flashed through my mind. I didn't want to make any more enemies, but I wasn't about to get myself killed to avoid it.

Before I could say anything else, there was a sudden, loud *Pop!*

Things around me shifted, and I felt something pulling me off the ground.

What the—?

I was snatched out of the world, thrown around in a colorless void, and dumped on a cold tile floor.

When I opened my eyes, I was surprised to see Dr. Bradley's smiling face above me. But any relief I might have felt disappeared when I caught sight of the Committee a few feet away.

"Let's get you up," said Dr. Bradley, helping me to my feet. He was holding the clunky cell phone he'd given me earlier. "When you didn't return, I knew something must have happened. I kept calling the phone until one of the lovely Committee members answered."

I was barely listening. Instead, I was frantically looking around for any sign of Klarr. If he'd found me in the Committee's waiting room before, what was to stop him from tracking me down again?

"What's the matter, Jenny?" said Dr. Bradley.

Klarr could be here any second! I mind-spoke—or rather, mind-screamed—at the doctor before remembering that he couldn't hear me. I did my best to mime Klarr's painted eyes and menacing smile.

"Not to worry," Dr. Bradley said, finally understanding. "Regrettably, Klarr must have been monitoring the portal I sent you through before. But the Committee members have since changed their location, and you were brought here with their magic. There is no chance Klarr could have followed you."

I wasn't convinced.

"I assure you, you're perfectly secure now," Dr. Bradley added. "I promise."

Was I really safe? The panic slowly faded, and I started thinking clearly again.

"I have good news!" said Dr. Bradley. "Your paperwork has gone through. The Committee can give you your mouth back."

Finally! I practically jumped up and clicked my heels together with joy.

"Come along." Dr. Bradley led me toward the long table and stood me in the center of the green circle.

"You have returned, Jennifer," the Committee said. "And we have received word that you were successful in your mission to retrieve Prince Lamb."

I nodded.

"You were?" said Dr. Bradley. "Why, that's wonderful news!"

"Unacceptable!" the Committee yelled at him.

Dr. Bradley blushed. "My sincerest apologies, dear members of the Committee. I won't speak out of turn again."

The women nodded in unison and turned back to me. "We are now authorized to return your mouth."

The Committee members picked up four identical pens with four identical hands and leaned forward to sign four identical pieces of paper. The moment they put down their pens, my face began to burn.

"Ah!"

I looked around before I realized that the sound had come from me. From my mouth. I had a mouth!

"It's back!" I ran my fingers over my mouth and bit my lips because I could. I'd never felt so happy to have a mouth before.

"Your mouth has been reinstated," the Committee said.

"Thank you!" I said, not even caring how unfair they'd been to me the last time I'd seen them. I turned to Dr. Bradley. "And thank you too! Oh, and before I forget, your mother called."

"My dear mum?" he said, his face brightening. "I haven't talked to her in ages!"

The Committee members loudly cleared their throats. "Jennifer. Now that we have the matter of your mouth settled, we must discuss your mission."

My excitement fizzled. "My mission? My mission is over. You said so yourselves. I rescued the prince."

"That was only part of your assignment," said the Committee. "Your main mission was to stop Klarr. You have not completed that task."

"Why can't you just use your magic to do it?" I said. "If you can give me my mouth back, why can't you give everyone in Speak theirs back too?"

"It is not about mouths," said the Committee. "If we reinstated everyone's mouths, Klarr would merely find another way to attack. He must be taken care of."

"Then take care of him!"

"Silence!" said the Committee. "We will not be given orders by a young adventurer. This mission was given to you, and you must complete it."

I glared at each of the women. "Says who?"

"It is in your contract."

"What contract?"

The Committee members waved their hands. A piece of paper floated toward me and unrolled itself. It was blank except for my name, written in green crayon. I stared, trying to figure out when I could have possibly signed it. And then I remembered. On that first day, more than three years earlier, when Anthony had appeared in my bedroom and offered to make me an adventurer, he'd had me write my name. "It's just a formality," he'd told me, smacking away on a piece of gum. And I'd trusted him.

"That's not a contract," I said. "It only has my name on it."

"The fine print is invisible," said the Committee, "but it is still binding. According to the contract, you agree to complete every adventure you are sent on. You cannot be released from it until you fulfill your obligation."

"But that's not fair. What about the last mission you sent me on? I didn't complete that one either. I was supposed to teach those unicorns about sharing, but they just chased me away."

"We are here to discuss your current mission," said the Committee. "According to our rules, you are contractually obligated to defeat Klarr."

"I didn't know what I was signing," I said. "You can't hold me to that."

"We can and we will."

"No!" I cried. "That crazy sorcerer's already tortured me and taken my mouth away. I'm not going anywhere near him again!"

The Committee members looked at each other in silence. I had the feeling no one had ever yelled at them before. But I didn't care. They couldn't make me go on a suicide mission.

"We are disappointed," they said finally. "We expected a lot from you, Jennifer. Your parents were the best adventurers we'd ever seen. We hoped you would be the greatest of all."

Chapter 11

I stared at the Committee, sure I'd heard wrong. "My what?"

"Your parents."

"What are you talking about?"

"My dear ladies," said Dr. Bradley, hobbling forward. "Perhaps this is not the best time to—"

"Unacceptable!"

Dr. Bradley pushed up his glasses. "But surely, it is too soon—"

"No, I want to hear this," I interrupted. My heart was drumming in my chest. I turned back to the Committee. "Are you saying my parents were adventurers?"

The women exchanged uncertain looks. "We should not have spoken of this."

"Tell me!" I said. "Who were they? What happened to them?"

The Committee members whispered among themselves

for a moment. Finally, they nodded in unison and turned back to me. "As we said, your parents were the greatest of adventurers. No one knows what became of them. They were on a mission when they disappeared. It is most regrettable."

"*Regrettable?*" How could they talk about my parents like they were a set of lost keys? "What mission? Why didn't anyone tell me?"

"It is classified information," said the Committee. "Released only to top-priority personnel."

"They're my parents! Doesn't that make me top priority?"

"You are too young," said the Committee. "Such information is only released after the age of eighteen."

"Why didn't anyone tell me?" I repeated. The giant room suddenly felt too small, and I could hardly breathe. How could any of what they'd said be true? All this time I'd thought my parents had just been normal people who'd mysteriously vanished, and now it turned out they'd disappeared because they'd been adventurers?

"Jenny," said Dr. Bradley, his voice low and sad. "I wanted desperately to tell you. But perhaps it was for the best. Think how upset you would have been if—"

"I'm upset right now! You lied to me! How could you

expect me to become an adventurer when adventuring made my parents disappear?"

"It wasn't his place to tell you," said the Committee. "It was not yet time."

"What gives you the right to decide something like that?"

"We are the Committee. If you are to be an adventurer, you will agree to follow our rules."

"Well, I don't agree to follow your rules anymore. If you don't tell me what happened to my parents, I'm never going on another adventure!"

The hall throbbed with stunned silence.

"You cannot threaten us in this manner," the Committee said finally. "You cannot simply quit. You signed the contract."

"Yes, I can." I grabbed the contract still hanging in the air and tore it in half. The Committee let out a collective gasp.

"Jenny, I implore you—" Dr. Bradley began.

"No!" I said. "I'm sick of having no friends and always getting hurt and following orders just because I'm told to. I don't want to be an adventurer anymore. I just want to be a normal girl." I ripped the contract in half again, and then again, until it was just a bunch of tiny pieces of paper.

Then I threw the pieces in the air and watched them fall around me like confetti.

"You have destroyed the contract!" said the Committee. "Your behavior is unacceptable! Unacceptable!"

An instant later, invisible hands dragged me away from the Committee's table. This time I didn't struggle. I couldn't have been happier to get away from the Committee. I never wanted to see those women again.

After the invisible hands dumped me on the floor of the waiting room, I scrambled to my feet. My head was pounding. I didn't even notice Anthony the Gnome sitting in one of the nearby chairs until his voice echoed through the room.

"There you are," he said, popping a jelly bean in his mouth. "That was taking forever."

I wanted to tear the jelly beans from his hands and mash them into nothing. How could he have tricked me into signing that contract? But just then Dr. Bradley opened the door and limped in.

"Thank goodness you're here, Anthony," he said. "Maybe you can talk some sense into her."

"About what?"

"I quit," I told him. "I tore up that fake contract you

made me sign, and I told the Committee I was done following their stupid rules."

Anthony gaped at me. For once, he seemed to be speechless.

"I've never seen the Committee members so angry," said Dr. Bradley.

"It's their fault for lying to me," I said. "Now, will one of you tell me what happened to my parents? What kind of mission were they on?"

Dr. Bradley shook his head. "I'm afraid we don't know. Their adventures were of the utmost secrecy. All I can tell you is that the magical worlds were greatly saddened when they didn't return."

Anthony nodded, his usual smile gone. "I must have eaten a wheelbarrow full of chocolate the day I found out. Your parents were the best."

I looked away. I didn't think I could stand to hear any more. "Please take me home."

"But leaving now would be a grave mistake," said Dr. Bradley. "The Committee might still be willing to accept your apology."

I almost laughed. "I don't have anything to apologize for. They're the ones who tricked me. Why should I work for them?"

"Because the magical worlds need you, Jenny. You're one of the most talented adventurers we've had in a long time."

"All I do is say cheesy things and get hurt by crazed unicorns and psycho sorcerers. Anyone could do that." I shook my head. "I'm done. Being an adventurer used to be fun. But now…" I didn't want to disappear like my parents had. I didn't want to go to a magical world and never come back. And I didn't want to be around people who lied to me. "I just want my normal life back."

"But, Jenny, it's not that simple," said Dr. Bradley.

"He's right, Jenny-girl. Why would you want to go back to your boring old life anyway? Your friends don't even remember who you are."

I blinked at him. "What did you say?"

The rosy color drained out of Anthony's cheeks. "Oh, um, I just mean—"

"What Anthony means is you've lost touch with them," Dr. Bradley interrupted. "It will be hard to make new friends after all this time."

"That's not what he said." I marched up to Anthony. "You said they don't remember who I am." I thought of the empty stares I always got from Melissa and Trish anytime

I tried to talk to them, and the way they'd act as if I were a complete stranger. What if they weren't mad at me? What if they really had no idea who I was? "What did you do to them?" I demanded.

Anthony gulped and looked to Dr. Bradley for help.

"Jenny," said the doctor. "Believe me, neither of us meant to—"

"Tell me!"

"We had to do it, Jenny-girl. Melissa and Trish heard you talking to me about one of your adventures. They knew way more than they should have. We needed to wipe their memories to make sure the magical worlds were kept secret."

"Please understand," said Dr. Bradley, "the Committee would never allow regular humans to know of other worlds. Your earth is very young and has yet to develop its own magic." He sighed before continuing, his voice barely above a whisper. "Our intention wasn't to make your friends forget you, just what they'd heard. But we must have miscalculated."

"So you took *all* their memories of me?"

Anthony stepped forward. "We tried to reverse the spell, but that didn't work."

"We hoped it would wear off in time, and it still may," Dr. Bradley added. "Sometimes something as simple as a sudden shock can reverse the spell."

I couldn't believe it. Had they been lying to me about everything? "So because the Committee is paranoid about the spread of magic, my friends can't have *any* memories of me?"

"Please believe that I am very sorry. And so is Anthony."

The gnome nodded. For once he looked genuinely concerned. But I didn't care how Anthony felt. I hated him. I hated them both.

"I want to go home right now," I said.

"But—"

"Take me home!"

Dr. Bradley gave a reluctant nod and looked at Anthony. The gnome sighed and snapped his fingers. *Pop!*

I was pulled out of the world, tossed around, and dumped onto my kitchen floor, alongside Anthony and Dr. Bradley.

As I got to my feet, Aunt Evie came into the room holding a mug of tea.

"Oh," she said, looking back and forth between the gnome and the doctor.

"It's all right, Aunt Evie. They're leaving."

"Jenny…" Dr. Bradley pleaded, but I shook my head. I didn't want to hear anything else he had to say.

"I'm done. It's over. I'm never going on an adventure again."

Dr. Bradley looked on the verge of begging, but Anthony gave him a pat on the shoulder. "Come on, old man. It's obvious we're not wanted here." Then he took Dr. Bradley's arm and led him out the door.

"Were those friends of yours?" asked Aunt Evie.

"No," I said. "Don't worry. They won't bother us anymore." Then I sank down at the kitchen table and put my head in my arms.

"Are you all right, kitten?" said Aunt Evie.

I shook my head, tears trickling onto my sleeves. Everything in my life had been a lie: my parents, my friends, Dr. Bradley. I had thought being an adventurer would be fun and exciting. Instead, it had taken everything I cared about away from me. And now I'd never get any of it back.

"There, there," said Aunt Evie, sitting down beside me and scratching the top of my head. "How about a nice saucer of warm milk?"

PART 2

PART 2

Chapter 12

Monday morning felt like the first day of school all over again. For once, I was going to arrive as a regular, normal girl. The last time I'd been so excited to get on the school bus had been in kindergarten on Halloween. Unfortunately, that had turned out to be a day of disappointment.

It was one of the few memories I had of my mother, even though I couldn't quite remember her face. She'd sewn me an Indiana Jones costume, complete with a whip made out of yarn. My mother had even pinned a plastic cobra to my sleeve so I could glance over at it and mutter, "I hate snakes!" To top it all off, I had secretly collected spiders for days and put them into a small jar.

When I'd arrived at school, I had swashbuckled my way into my classroom, released the spiders onto the floor, and started saving my classmates from certain doom. The day had ended in the principal's office, and I hadn't been a fan of Halloween, or school, ever since. A few months later, my parents had disappeared, and I'd had no one to make costumes for me anymore.

But today would be different, I told myself. It wouldn't end in disappointment.

Before I left the house, I took a few practice swings with my mini-golf club to help calm my nerves. My injured arm was finally back to normal, and my favorite pink ball sailed into the cup like it couldn't wait to go in. That had to be a lucky sign, I decided as I slipped the ball into my pocket. Today would be the first day of the rest of my amazingly average life.

When I got on the bus, no one said a word to me, which wasn't unusual. But they also stared at me like I was some kind of sea monster. I sat in a seat by myself and tried to ignore the strange looks. When I got to homeroom, the staring continued. I wasn't sure what was wrong. Did I have a tarantula on my head? Or had I gotten so good at being invisible over the past three years that everyone was surprised to see me?

When the teacher came in, she scanned the room, humming under her breath. But when her eyes stopped on me, her face changed. She looked down at the list in her hand and studied it carefully.

"Are you new, dear?" the teacher asked finally.

I stared back at her, not sure what to say.

She raised her eyebrows and walked over to my desk. "Dear?" she asked again. "Are you new?"

I swallowed. "I'm Jenny." The other kids gave me curious looks, as if I really was the new girl. What was going on?

"Is today your first day?" the teacher tried again. Clearly, she was flagging the new girl as a dummy.

"I guess so," I said finally.

"You'll have to go to the office. I don't have you on my list."

"Oh...okay." I stood up, feeling like my head weighed twice as much as usual.

"Trish?" said the teacher. "Can you show our new student the way to the office?"

Trish nodded and hopped up from her desk. I wanted to yell that I knew the way to the office, that I knew every part of the school! But I clamped my mouth shut and let Trish lead me out into the hallway. I didn't know what was happening. Had Anthony and Dr. Bradley done something to *everyone* at my school?

"Where did you move from?" Trish asked as we walked along. Her voice seemed higher than I remembered it, like she'd swallowed a squeaky toy. I had to take a deep breath before I could answer. It still hurt that my once best friend had no idea who I was.

"California," I said.

"Cool!" Trish squealed. "Do you know any famous actors?"

"Um, no."

Trish's face fell. "Oh. Well, this place is really boring. You'll be begging your parents to take you back to your old school by the end of the week."

I swallowed hard. My parents. If no one remembered who I was, I'd have to explain that I didn't have a normal family like they all did. But how was I supposed to tell people that my parents had disappeared in some magical kingdom and that my aunt was better at talking to animals than to humans?

Finally, we came to the main office. I went up to the secretary, hoping that this had all been some big misunderstanding and that the entire school hadn't forgotten me.

"Can I help you?" the secretary asked.

"Hi. I guess I'm new."

She gave me a blank look for a moment. Then her eyes lit up. "Are you Jenny?"

"Yes!"

"Your grandfather said you would be coming in today." She searched through a pile of papers on her desk.

"My grandfather?"

"Yes, he came in earlier this morning and said you would be joining us."

"He did?" Of course the secretary had to mean Dr. Bradley.

"He left a note for you." She handed me a small, cream envelope. "And I have your old school records here somewhere…"

I took a deep breath and opened the envelope. The letter was written in fancy ancient-looking script, the kind that you'd find on a scroll.

Dear Jenny,

I must apologize once again for using magic on those close to you. Over the years Anthony and I were forced to use a Distraction Powder on your teachers and classmates to make your absences less noticeable. The powder is generally harmless, but when the dosage is suddenly stopped, it often causes a lapse in memory. I am sorry to say it may prove to be permanent. However, I hope you look upon this as a chance to begin anew at your school, to create the magic-free life you desire.

Sincerest apologies,

Dr. Bartholomew Bradley

I realized suddenly how blind I'd been. I'd thought a side effect of magic was that normal people just naturally forgot the strange things they'd seen. But Dr. Bradley and Anthony had been altering everyone's minds all along. I'd been so wrapped up in my adventures that I hadn't noticed all the things the doctor and Anthony had been doing behind my back.

"Your grandfather is such a sweet old man," the secretary was saying. "It's a shame he has to go into a nursing home, but I guess we all have our time. Ah, here they are!" The secretary dug out a few pieces of paper. She studied them intently, copying down some information onto a form. When I looked at my "old school records," I was amazed to find that the pieces of paper were absolutely blank. Apparently, there was no end to Dr. Bradley's magic.

"Here's your class schedule," said the secretary finally. I looked at the yellow piece of paper and smirked. My schedule was no different than it had been the week before. "Good luck," she added with a warm smile.

"Thanks."

As I turned to go, Trish fell in step beside me. Walking down the hall with her almost made me feel like I had my old life back. Too bad Trish had no idea that we'd both had chicken pox in second grade or that we'd once colored our hair with permanent marker, or all the other things that had been erased from her memory. If those things only existed in my head, then maybe we really were total strangers.

"Do you want to come over after school today and watch TV?" Trish asked after a minute. "You can meet my friend Melissa."

I couldn't help smiling. "Sure!" Maybe things weren't so bad after all. This was my chance to get my old friends back and maybe even make some new ones. I could finally catch up on all I'd missed the past few years.

"Then you can tell us all about California!" Trish squeaked.

My smile disappeared. Was I really going to have to spend the rest of my life lying about who I was?

Chapter 13

"Jenny, do you want to come over and watch TV with us this weekend?" asked Trish.

I zipped up my bulging backpack and heaved it over my shoulder. I'd only been back at school a few days, and already I was swamped with homework. I fell in step between Trish and Melissa as we headed to the buses.

"Again?" I tried to keep the disappointment out of my voice. I didn't dislike watching TV, but that was all Melissa and Trish ever wanted to do. They didn't even chat or joke around while they watched. They stared at the screen with their mouths open, like they were trying to drink in every image they saw. Sometimes I would get so bored that I'd count how many times they blinked while they were watching. It was a disturbingly low number.

"Don't you want to hang out with us?" said Melissa, her face falling. Her eyes, though, were as empty as ever. I couldn't remember them being that way before, but now they always seemed blank. Was that yet another side effect of Dr. Bradley's magic?

"Of course I want to hang out with you guys!" I said. What was wrong with me? I had wanted my old friends back, and now I had them. Why couldn't I be happy with that?

But the problem was that I couldn't help remembering how much more fun my friends used to be. When we'd been younger, the three of us had acted out our favorite fairy tales and written funny poems about each another. Trish had dragged us to the library to sniff all the musty old books, and Melissa had made us listen to the songs she'd learned in her voice lessons. I'd been the one to plan little challenges for us, like seeing who could make her family members say "cantaloupe" the most times in one day. (I never won those sorts of challenges since I just had Aunt Evie, but they were still fun to invent.)

I knew we were too old to do some of those things now, but did that mean we had to watch silly TV shows in absolute silence for hours on end? Even when we weren't watching TV, all Trish and Melissa wanted to talk about were actors and actresses I'd never heard of. It was like they didn't care about their own lives, only about the fictional ones they saw on TV.

"Melissa, do you sing?" I not-so-subtly asked as we walked by the main office. The secretary gave me a wave, but I pretended not to see her. I didn't need her asking me about my "grandfather" again.

Melissa shrugged. "I used to, but it started taking up too much of my time."

"Yeah," Trish squeaked. "She was never around to hang out."

"So what did you do when you were by yourself?" I asked Trish.

She thought for a moment. "I read a lot," she said. I almost smiled until she added, "But it was making me miss my shows, so I stopped."

I sighed. What had happened to my friends? Unless they'd been abducted by aliens, I just couldn't believe they were the same girls. Maybe memory dust was more harmful than Dr. Bradley had let on.

"Hey, I know!" said Trish. "We can come watch TV at your house this weekend, Jenny. We still haven't seen where you live."

"And don't say no," said Melissa. "We don't care if you're not done unpacking yet."

What was I supposed to do? I couldn't exactly invite my "new" friends over to my house since I didn't actually have the parents I kept talking about. I knew I should have just told Trish and Melissa the truth from the beginning, but for a while, at least, it had been nice to pretend I was just like them.

"I think my dad's planning on painting the living room," I said finally, hating myself for yet another lie. "He wouldn't want us in the way."

Melissa shrugged. "Okay, then we'll go to my house."

I said good-bye to my friends and hopped onto the bus. After I found an empty seat and plopped down, I couldn't shake the icky feeling in the pit of my stomach. Was having a regular life supposed to be this hard? Or was I just doing it wrong?

Suddenly something white darted past the bus window. I sat up. Was it a fairy? Or worse, a unicorn?

Then I saw what it was: a plastic bag. The wind blew and the bag drifted away.

Great, I was losing it. Maybe I should have made Dr. Bradley sprinkle *me* with memory dust. Then I could stop looking for things that weren't there and be happy with the things that were.

But I *was* happy, I told myself. This was exactly what I wanted. To be normal.

The bus rolled along, eventually going past Dr. Bradley's old house. Or at least what *used* to be his house. It looked more deserted and run-down than ever with heaps of other people's garbage piled up in the yard.

Where was he now? Monitoring someone else on his puddle screen? Feeding some other adventurer batches of homemade butterscotch pudding?

Not that I cared. I was just fine never seeing that crazy doctor ever again. Not after he'd…But the trouble was that it was getting harder to remember the bad things he'd done when there had been so many good. Yes, Dr. Bradley had taken my friends from me, but now I wasn't sure if they were as great as I remembered them being. And he'd kept my parents' true identities a secret, but what little he had been able to tell me didn't give me enough to be able to find them.

But the worst part was that Dr. Bradley had really been my friend. For three years I'd told him all about my adventures, and he had listened and smiled and joked with me. Now that he was gone, all I had were memories. Even Anthony, as crazy as he'd made me, had at least shared some of those experiences with me. With no one to talk to about them, it was almost like my adventures had never happened. All I had were the treasure chests in my closet, and those weren't exactly great at conversation.

The bus pulled up to my house. When I unlocked the front door, I was almost bowled over by an angry goose trying to escape. I managed to grab it by the tail before it ran out the door.

As I finally finished wrestling the goose back inside, feathers flying, I heard an unfamiliar voice call out from down the hall. "Jenny?" it said.

I turned to see an amazingly cute boy standing in my living room. Everything from his hair to his clothes to his lopsided grin was straight out of an ad for suntan lotion. And yet there was something familiar about him.

"Do I know you?" My backpack slipped out of my hand and fell to the floor.

The boy laughed. "Jenny, it's me. Prince Lamb."

I blinked. Besides the boy's grin, there was nothing sheepish about him. His skin, which had once been mayonnaise-colored, now glowed with a flawless tan. His curly mop was carefully slicked and gelled. And his clothes were catalog-perfect.

"You have a mouth!" I managed to say when I could breathe again.

Prince Lamb nodded. "The Committee worked some of its magic this morning. I would never fit into your world without a mouth."

"But you look so different. What happened to you?"

Prince Lamb's grin widened. "Ribba gave me a makeover."

Wow. Ribba really was good at the whole stylist thing. Even Prince Lamb's voice sounded different than it had when I'd heard it in my head. It was stronger and more confident now.

"But what are you *doing* here?" I asked. "Aren't you…mad at me?"

The prince's forehead wrinkled. "Why would I be angry with you?"

"Well." I felt my cheeks getting hot. "I did kind of let your kingdom down. You know, by not defeating Klarr and all of that."

"Ah," said Prince Lamb. "Well, you don't need to worry about that, Jenny. I understand your decision."

"You do? It didn't seem that way before."

"At first I was angry," he admitted. "But then I realized you were right. You did what you could, and it was someone else's turn to try."

"And you guys figured it out, right? You found a way to beat Klarr?"

The prince hesitated. "Well, no. The sorcerer struck back and has been destroying the kingdom of Speak, bit by bit. But I am sure it is only a matter of time before he's stopped."

"Wait. Your kingdom is under attack, and you came *here*?"

"I wanted to stay and fight, but Mother begged the Committee to take me somewhere safe so Klarr couldn't kidnap me again. It took a few days for the paperwork to go through, but the Committee members finally decided to send me here. They figured I'd be all right in a non-magical world."

"I'm sorry," I said, knowing it was partly my fault that his world was no longer safe.

"I'm sure my mother will find a solution. And who knows, I might decide I like living among humans."

"But you're a prince. You can't just walk away from that."

Prince Lamb shrugged. "You walked away from being an adventurer."

"Yeah, but you were born a prince. That means it's for life."

"You were born an adventurer." Prince Lamb crossed his arms in front of his chest. I noticed his shirt sleeves were perfectly cuffed at his wrists like someone out of a magazine. Somehow that was one of the most annoying things I'd ever seen.

"Okay, so you want to be a human. Why come to me?"

"I was hoping you could show me how it's done."

I laughed. "If I find out, I'll let you know."

"Come on, Jenny. We're friends. Won't you help me?"

His pleading eyes pierced into me. Of all the creatures I had met in my travels, Prince Lamb was the first one to seek me out afterward. The others had just said their good-byes and forgotten me like a bad song. But Prince Lamb had wanted to see me again. And he needed my help, not because I was a hero but because I was a regular girl.

"Do you mean it?" I asked. "Are we really friends?"

The prince gave me a lopsided grin. "Of course we are."

How could I turn him down? I wasn't exactly swimming in friends these days. But more than that, I felt like I owed Prince Lamb after abandoning his kingdom. If I couldn't defeat Klarr, at least I could help the prince by giving him a place to hide out.

"Okay, fine," I said. "But I'm done with all that magical stuff. So while you're here, you have to act like a totally normal human."

Prince Lamb nodded eagerly. "Of course."

"And you can't tell anyone who you really are, okay? One slipup and the Committee will spray everybody with memory dust. I can't let that happen again. Got it?"

"Yes," said Prince Lamb, holding his hands up in surrender. "I'll do whatever you say, Jenny. I promise."

I tried to tell myself that I was doing the right thing, that Prince Lamb needed my help. But as much as I wanted to believe that I was making the right decision, I couldn't help wondering if maybe I was making a huge mistake.

Chapter 14

I'd always been a little jealous of how much attention Aunt Evie paid to her animal patients. But after seeing her fawn all over Prince Lamb at dinner that first night, I realized I'd been lucky my aunt had been a little oblivious to me over the years.

"Are you sure you don't want me to cut up your broccoli for you?" Aunt Evie asked as she hovered over Prince Lamb's plate. Maybe she could somehow sense that he was a lamb at heart.

"Thank you," the prince said. "I think I can manage."

Considering this was the prince's first meal ever, he was doing better than managing. It took him a few tries to get into the swing of chewing, but soon he was munching away like a pro. As I watched him savoring every bite, I tried to imagine what it would be like to taste food for the first time.

"This meal is…" Prince Lamb searched for the word. "Delicious."

Aunt Evie beamed as she went back to her seat. "Just wait until you try my kibble brownies!" She turned to me. "Your friend is such a gentleman."

I had to admit that Aunt Evie was right. Even though his table manners weren't perfect—and who could blame him after he'd only had a mouth for a day!—the prince was an excellent guest. I assumed that came from a lifetime of preparing to be king one day.

"So how long will you be in town, Prince?" said Aunt Evie.

I swallowed a giggle. Only my aunt wouldn't notice that "Prince" was an unusual name.

"As long as you'll have me," said Prince Lamb.

Aunt Evie looked puzzled.

"Didn't I tell you?" I chimed in. "Prince is staying with us. He's a, um, new exchange student."

"Oh, how lovely!" said Aunt Evie. "Maybe we'll learn a new language." She leaned down and slipped a piece of broccoli to a raccoon that was rubbing up against her leg.

The doorbell rang.

"I'll get it," I said, jumping to my feet. The only people

who came by unannounced were girl scouts selling cookies or boy scouts raising money for field trips. Aunt Evie would usually "donate" a bag of birdseed and send them on their way. I liked to save the poor kids from having to drag the unwanted bags all the way home.

But when I opened the door, I was stunned at the sight of the two visitors on my front steps.

"Surprise!" Trish squealed.

"What are you guys doing here?" I asked.

"We wanted to help you unpack and decorate!" said Melissa. "It'll be a way to celebrate the end of your first week here."

"Oh…thanks. But it's not really a good time right now."

Melissa's smile disappeared. "Look, Jenny," she said, giving Trish a sideways glance. "We don't know you that well, but it seems like you're hiding something."

What could I say? I couldn't tell them the truth, or some member of the Committee would swoop in and erase their memories again. But I couldn't stand to lie anymore. Ever since I'd reintroduced myself to Melissa and Trish, I'd done nothing but compare them to how they used to be. But now I realized that I had changed too. The old Jenny would never have lied to her best friends.

"Well—" I began.

"Oh my gosh!" Trish squeaked, her eyes focusing on something behind me.

Melissa also appeared stunned. "He looks like a soap-opera star," she whispered.

I turned to see Prince Lamb standing behind me, looking cuter than even the most popular boys at school.

"Melissa, Trish, this is—"

"I'm Prince," Prince Lamb broke in. He came forward and shook hands with Trish and Melissa. They both looked like they might faint.

"Prince like the singer?" said Trish.

"Prince like the monarch," Prince Lamb answered. He ran his hand through his sculpted hair, half closing his eyes as he did it. I could almost picture Ribba coaching him on that move.

"Oh," said Trish, blinking rapidly.

"He's my cousin," I said, racking up yet another lie. "He's visiting."

"From California?" asked Melissa. Her blank eyes were so wide, I was afraid they might actually fall out of her head.

"Yes," I jumped in as Prince Lamb started to answer.

"Do you know any famous actors?" said Trish. She practically had drool dribbling down her chin.

Prince Lamb's face lit up. "Actually, I do know this one frog—"

"No one you would've heard of," I jumped in again.

"How long are you here for, Prince?" asked Melissa. She tossed her hair over her shoulder in a way she'd probably gotten from a TV show.

"For as long as they'll have me." The prince gave a little wink, and I saw Melissa shiver.

"So you'll be in school with us?" Trish shrieked.

"No," I said just as Prince Lamb gave an eager nod.

"Of course I'll be attending your school," he said. "I wouldn't have it otherwise." He turned and gave me a meaningful look.

I wanted to object. What if the prince's identity was discovered and the Committee brainwashed my entire school again? But as Prince Lamb looked at me, all I could do was nod. Maybe it was crazy, but I'd told him I would help. As much as I wanted to, I knew I couldn't back out on another promise.

"Who's at the door?" Aunt Evie called from the hall. I tried to block the doorway, but it was too late.

"Oh, is that your mom?" said Trish.

"We want to meet her!" said Melissa, pushing me out of the way.

Before I could stop them, they were inside and face-to-face with Aunt Evie.

"Hello," my aunt said uncertainly, looking like a cornered mouse.

"Hi, I'm Melissa."

"And I'm Trish." She grabbed Aunt Evie's hand and shook it like a baby rattle. "It's so nice to finally meet you!" She glanced over at me. "Is your dad around too?"

Aunt Evie cocked her head to the side. "Oh my," she said to Trish. "I'm afraid you're a little confused. Jenny's father has been gone for years."

Trish's face fell. "But I thought…"

Melissa spun around to face me, her eyes narrowing. "You said you lived with both of your parents."

I swallowed. "Um…"

"She used to," said Aunt Evie. "But that was a long time ago, when she was just a puppy. No one has seen them in years." She clicked her tongue and shook her head like it was all such a pity.

"Wait," said Trish. "So you're not Jenny's mom?"

"Oh no," said Aunt Evie. "I'm her father's sister. I'm afraid I'm not very good with children."

I looked down at my feet, but I could feel Trish and Melissa's eyes burning into the top of my head. I didn't know how to go about trying to explain.

"Would anyone like some dinner?" Prince Lamb chimed in. His words did nothing to break up the suffocating tension in the room.

"No thanks," Trish said coldly. "Come on, Melissa."

"Good-bye, Jenny. If that's even your real name," Melissa spat.

My two best friends stormed out of the house, slamming the door behind them. Time seemed to stop. What had I done? There was no way Melissa and Trish would ever believe anything I said now. I'd thought losing them the first time had been hard. But losing them again hurt a hundred times more.

Chapter 15

On Monday morning, I woke up to the smell of pancakes. I was still in a bad mood from everything that had happened with Melissa and Trish the other night, but this was Prince Lamb's first day of school and I was determined to make it a good one. I threw on some clothes and rushed down to the kitchen. Prince Lamb was already at the table, stuffing his mouth full of breakfast.

"Good morning!" said Aunt Evie. She had a muskrat perched on her head and another one on her shoulder as she set a pancake-filled plate in front of me.

"These smell good," I said. My aunt rarely remembered to cook more than one meal in a row. Having the prince around definitely had its advantages.

"And they're crunchy," said Prince Lamb.

"Crunchy?" I inspected one of the pancakes and found something that looked suspiciously like a pellet of rabbit food. I shrugged and poured a bunch of maple syrup on top before digging in. It tasted pretty good.

"Are you excited about your first day at Jenny's school?" Aunt Evie asked.

"Absolutely," said Prince Lamb. "But I doubt it will be as much fun as spending time with those two muskrats."

Aunt Evie giggled as she scratched the animals' heads. "They're a feisty duo," she said. "I just hope I can help them work through their sibling rivalry."

"How close are they in age?" asked Prince Lamb.

"Well…" Aunt Evie launched into a long explanation of the difference between muskrat years and people years.

I stared as the prince and my aunt chatted away as if they'd known each other forever. I couldn't remember a single time I'd talked to my aunt about her job. It had always seemed so foreign to me, just as school seemed like another world to Aunt Evie.

After breakfast was done and Prince Lamb and I had helped clean up the kitchen, it was time for school.

"Ready for your first day?" I asked.

"Of course!" said Prince Lamb. He grabbed the old schoolbag I'd lent him (he wasn't bothered by the pink hearts and purple stars), and we headed to the bus stop.

"If you don't stop grinning like a fool," I told him, "you're going to get beat up."

"Bleat up?" asked the prince.

"*Beat* up," I said with a laugh. "Meaning picked on. All the girls might swoon over you, but I doubt the boys will."

"Don't worry," said Prince Lamb. "I've been trained in the art of charming people since birth. That is what princes do, after all."

When we got to school, I brought Prince Lamb to the front office, praying no one would ask too many questions. I shouldn't have worried. Prince Lamb's charm went into full swing. Within a few minutes he had a class schedule and something like a lunch date with the secretary.

"Aren't you just the nicest boy?" she said, shaking her head in wonder. "If only all the boys had your manners!"

Prince Lamb beamed.

"You hang on to this one," the secretary told me with a wink. I blushed. "Have you had a chance to see your grandfather?" she added.

I shuffled my feet. "Not really."

"I know it's easy to forget about your grandparents when you're young. But I'm sure it would brighten his day to see you."

"Yeah," I said, pulling Prince Lamb away.

"Who was she talking about?" he asked when we were out in the hallway again.

"Dr. Bradley."

"You miss him, don't you?" Prince Lamb said with a sympathetic look.

In a moment of weakness the day before, I'd told the prince all about what had happened with Dr. Bradley. Now I regretted ever opening my mouth.

"No," I said. "All he did was lie to me. Why would I miss that?"

"I'm sure he had no choice," said Prince Lamb.

"People always have a choice," I said, sounding like a character out of a bad movie. I tapped the side of my head, hoping to finally shut off the corny chip in my brain. Then I turned to Prince Lamb. "Ready for class?"

The prince nodded, and for a moment he looked like an eager sheep. Then he pushed up his cuffed sleeves, and he was more boy-suave than ever.

When we walked into the loud classroom, it went instantly silent. Everyone watched as the prince and I sat down. It reminded me of the first time I had seen the inhabitants of Speak, with their wide, examining eyes.

Trish and Melissa were whispering together in the corner. They didn't even bother looking my way, and I didn't blame them. I wouldn't want to be friends with a big, fat liar either.

"We have a new student joining us today," the teacher said. "His name is…Prince Lamb?"

The prince shot up from his seat and trotted to the front of the room. "That is correct, madam," he said. "I am Prince. And it is a pleasure to make all of your acquaintances."

All eyes in the room stared back at him in surprise. There went his chances of ever being accepted.

"I have recently moved here from, er, California," the prince went on. "I like spending time out of doors, especially taking long walks through grassy fields. I am very fond of all types of music, enjoy trying new things, and am an excellent listener."

There was dead silence as Prince Lamb went back to his seat. I could almost hear people's brains churning.

Then, to my utter surprise, I saw dreamy smiles spread across the girls' faces. Meanwhile, the boys were sizing the prince up like he was their competition. I had to bite the inside of my cheek to keep from laughing. If they only knew he was going to grow up to be a sheep!

Finally, it was lunchtime. I gripped my bagged lunch

tightly and made my way over to the table I'd shared with Trish and Melissa the previous week.

"Hi, guys," I said.

They looked up at me but didn't say anything.

"I don't blame you for being mad. I just wanted to say I'm sorry."

Melissa chewed on her lip. "We don't forgive you," she said. "But we have a question."

"Okay."

"All the girls have been asking about Prince," said Trish. "Do you know if he has a girlfriend back home?"

I fought back a smile. "I don't think so."

Trish and Melissa exchanged excited looks. Then they turned their noses away from me.

I sighed and went over to an empty table in the corner of the cafeteria. Back in my adventurer days, I'd mostly sat by myself and hadn't really minded being alone. So why did it feel so awful now?

As I took out my sandwich, Prince Lamb emerged from the lunch line with a tray balanced in his hands. He was surrounded by a group of the most popular boys in the entire school. I could only stare as they worked their way over to my table.

"Jenny," said Prince Lamb, leaning in to whisper in my ear. "Is it all right if these fellows sit with us?"

"Um, okay. You sure make friends fast."

He gave me a devilish grin. "They seemed impressed with my ability to eat an entire stack of napkins."

"You're kidding."

Prince Lamb raised his eyebrows mysteriously. "Lads, do you all know Jenny?" he said to his group of followers. "She's, er, my cousin."

"Hey." I tried to pretend like I hung out with popular boys all the time, but the crazy smile on my face probably gave me away.

A few of the boys gave me polite nods as they sat down, but most just ignored me. Clearly, they were only interested in new kids who could eat stacks of paper products.

"Prince, how do you get your shirt to look like that?" one of the boys asked.

Prince Lamb glanced down at his perfectly cuffed sleeves. "It's simple, really." He did a demonstration while all the other boys leaned in, studying his every move. They reminded me of a flock of sheep. Maybe that was why they'd taken to Prince Lamb so quickly.

I knew being jealous was silly, but it just didn't seem

fair. From the second Prince Lamb had set foot in my world, he had managed to do everything right. Aunt Evie paid more attention to him than she ever had to me, and Prince Lamb was more popular after a few hours than I had been my entire life. The prince had asked me for help, but the truth was he didn't need it at all. In fact, he was better at being normal than I'd ever be.

Chapter 16

"Are you sure you don't want to come get ice cream with us?" Prince Lamb asked after school a few days later. "It'll be fun."

Over the prince's shoulder I could see his entire flock of friends glaring at me. They didn't want me to come with them; they just wanted me to stop hogging their new fearless leader.

"I have a lot of homework to do," I said. I knew he was only inviting me out of pity, and I had no desire to be the loser tagalong "cousin."

Prince Lamb gave a little shrug and headed over to his herd of friends. He couldn't seem to quit being a ruler no matter where he went. I was disgusted to see that all the boys in the group now wore their shirt sleeves cuffed just like Prince Lamb.

I hopped onto the school bus and settled into my usual seat. Had being a regular girl been this hard before I'd become an adventurer? I didn't think so. But then again, all the things that made me a good adventurer had been okay when I was younger. I'd always had a big imagination, running around the neighborhood on made-up missions. And I'd loved taking charge and telling people what to do. But if I tried to do any of those things now, the other kids would think I was a bossy weirdo.

I would just have to find some other way to fit in, I decided. Would it be wrong to crack open my treasure chests and pay kids in gold pieces to be friends with me?

As the bus sputtered through my neighborhood, my glazed-over eyes suddenly widened in disbelief. I leaned forward and stared out the window.

Dr. Bradley's house, always dark and gloomy, suddenly looked bright and cheerful. The trash piles were gone, and someone had painted the door and shutters lollipop pink. A gardener was ripping out tangled weeds and replacing them with tulips.

The moment the bus came to a stop, I raced down the street.

"What are you doing?" I yelled at the startled gardener.

"Just got hired to clean this place up a bit," he said. "Before the new people move in next week."

"What people?" The feeling developing in my stomach was almost as sickening as the new door color.

"I don't know," the man answered with a friendly smile. "But I hear they have kids. Maybe you'll have some new friends in the neighborhood."

My knees went wobbly.

"You okay?" the gardener asked.

"No," I said. Then I turned and fled back down the street.

What had I expected? That Dr. Bradley would keep secretly living in the house and watching over me?

I stopped in mid-step. That's exactly what I'd thought. As much as I wanted to pretend I was happy with Dr. Bradley out of my life, a part of me hadn't believed he was really gone. But now there was no denying it. Some happy, bubbly family would be coming to take over his house, and I would have to watch them all pile into their minivan, decked out in "I heart mini-golf" T-shirts.

The thought made my feet start up again. I went faster and faster until I was almost running. I unlocked the front door of Aunt Evie's house and threw it open, ready to bolt up the stairs and fling myself onto my bed.

But Aunt Evie was standing in the hallway, an iguana

cradled in her arms. "Jenny," she said in surprise. "What are you doing here?"

I slammed the door shut behind me. "I live here, remember?"

"Well, of course, you live here," said Aunt Evie. "Where's Prince?"

"Off with his friends."

"Oh good." She smiled. "He's a sweet boy. He deserves nice friends."

"And I don't?" The words were like venom coming out of my mouth.

"What do you mean?" asked Aunt Evie. "You have friends. What about those girls who came by last week?"

"They're not my friends anymore, thanks to you. If you hadn't told them the truth about my parents, they wouldn't hate me right now."

Aunt Evie blinked. "What was I supposed to tell them?"

"I don't know! But you ruined everything!"

"I'm sorry…I had no idea."

"Of course you didn't, because you don't know anything about me. You care more about Prince than you do about me!"

Aunt Evie's mouth fell open. "That's not true."

"Don't even try to deny it!" I said. "You wish I was more like him but I'm not, and there's nothing I can do about it." I pushed past Aunt Evie and darted up the stairs. I slammed my bedroom door shut and threw myself on the bed. Before I knew it, I was sobbing uncontrollably for the first time in years. The last time had been on the day Aunt Evie had come to get me from school and tell me that my parents were missing. I felt just as alone as I had that day…and just as hopeless.

• • •

That evening, as I lay spread out on my bed tossing my pink mini-golf ball up in the air, there was a gentle knock on the door. I'd been locked up in my room ever since the fight with Aunt Evie. I wasn't mad anymore, just tired and sad and hungry.

"Jenny?" Prince Lamb's voice came through the door. "Can I come in?"

As much as I wanted to, I couldn't hide forever. "Okay."

The door creaked open, and the prince popped his head in. He took a few hesitant steps into my room, like he was afraid I'd claw his face off.

"It's all right," I said, putting the mini-golf ball on my nightstand. "Sit down."

Prince Lamb perched on the edge of my bed and gave me a sympathetic smile. "Are you all right?" he asked.

"I guess. Aunt Evie probably told you what I said to her."

"She didn't go into details, but she seemed rather upset."

I wouldn't have been surprised if my aunt hated me for what I'd said. Yes, Aunt Evie could be distracted, but she did the best she could. It wasn't fair for me to yell at her like that.

"What happened?" asked Prince Lamb.

"I don't know. I guess I was just fed up with everything."

"Like what?"

I thought for a minute, trying to find a way to explain. "Well, when I first became an adventurer, I thought my life would be great. But then things didn't turn out the way I wanted. So I thought becoming an average girl was the solution. But that didn't work out either. I'm just not good at being anything, I guess."

"That's not true," said Prince Lamb. "You're good at *everything*."

"Um, hardly." My only talent these days seemed to be messing things up.

"Jenny, you're one of the bravest creatures I know. And you're good at solving problems."

"Maybe other people's, but not my own."

"What sorts of problems?" said the prince.

I pulled my knees up to my chest. "Like the fact that no one likes me," I said. "Don't even try to deny it. I've lived in the same house as Aunt Evie for years, and I think she's talked to you more in the past few days than she's ever talked to me."

"If that's true, it's not because she likes me better," said Prince Lamb, shaking his head.

"Yes, it is. You're just likeable."

Prince Lamb laughed. "Trust me, it's all an act. If you wanted to, you could do it too."

"How?"

"Well, your aunt's not comfortable around people. I could see that when I first met her. But she loves animals, so I asked her about them."

"I don't know anything about animals," I said.

"And your aunt doesn't know anything about being an adventurer or being a twelve-year-old girl. But that doesn't mean you can never speak to each other. You just have to meet somewhere in the middle. Ask her questions. Take some time to familiarize yourself with her interests."

"You sound like an advice column."

Prince Lamb laughed again and pushed up his shirt sleeves. "Ribba did have me read a few of those as part of my makeover. But this isn't something I learned from a magazine. It's what I've had to do my entire life as a prince."

Could he possibly be right? For years I'd been afraid that the real reason Aunt Evie didn't know how to talk to me was because she didn't like me. What if she saw me as a burden her brother had dumped on her? But maybe Aunt Evie just had no idea how to relate to a girl like me.

"I guess I could try to take an interest in her patients a little more," I said. "As long as they don't try to pee on me."

"I think that sounds reasonable," said Prince Lamb, getting to his feet. "Your aunt had some work to finish up tonight, but she left dinner out for you in case you're hungry."

I stood up, surprised at my sudden urge to hug him. I guess we really were friends. "Thanks," I said. "For everything."

"That's what friends are for," said Prince Lamb with a cheesy smile.

"Hey, I'm the one who's supposed to say stuff like that!" I said, jokingly elbowing his side.

"Hmm," said Prince Lamb, pretending to think it over. "Maybe I should become an adventurer."

I couldn't help laughing as I followed Prince Lamb

down the stairs. "Don't let Anthony hear you say that.
He'll come whisk you away!"

I tried to laugh again, but thinking about Anthony made
something stab at my chest. Missing him and Dr. Bradley
was pointless. Yes, they'd been big parts of my life for years,
but all that was over now. It was time to finally move on.

Chapter 17

The next morning, I found my aunt sitting at the kitchen table and stirring a plate-sized cup of tea.

"Good morning," I said softly.

"Hello, dear," said Aunt Evie, peering down into her teacup. I knew she didn't want to look me in the eyes for fear that I'd start another fight. That was what animals did to avoid conflict.

"Where's Prince?" I asked.

"He left early, said he had some things to do. He didn't even want breakfast, but I gave him a few dog biscuits to take with him."

"Oh good." I sat down at the table. Apologies weren't really my thing, but this one needed to be done. "Aunt Evie, I'm really sorry about what I said yesterday. I didn't mean it."

"It's all right," she said, stirring her tea again. "I know things haven't been easy for you."

"But that's not an excuse for me to take it out on you."

Aunt Evie let out a long sigh and looked up at me. "Don't worry, dear. It's water under the fishbowl." She smiled sadly. "You know, you are so much like your father. He was always so determined, just charging through life, never afraid of anything. But sometimes that made him feel a bit lonely."

"Really?" It was rare for my aunt to talk about either of my parents. I think bringing them up made her even sadder than it made me.

"Oh yes," said Aunt Evie. "And he was never very fond of my animals."

I glanced down at the duck waddling through the kitchen. "It's not that I'm not fond of them," I said. "I just don't really know what to do with them."

"Animals are easy!" said Aunt Evie. "Ducks, for example, only want to be tickled." She reached out and tickled under the duck's bill. It let out an angry quack, and Aunt Evie giggled. "See?"

"Are you sure they like that?" I said as the duck hurried out of the kitchen.

"Oh yes, almost as much as they like eating peanut butter."

"I'll have to remember that." I glanced at the clock. "I guess I should get going."

"Okay, dear," said Aunt Evie, giving me another smile. "Have fun with the other chicks."

"Thanks, Aunt Evie." I bent down and gave my aunt a kiss on the cheek for the first time in ages. "I'll try."

• • •

At lunch that day, I sat with Prince Lamb and his friends and attempted to laugh at their jokes. But no matter how hard I tried, I just couldn't find squirting ketchup up someone else's nose funny.

Finally, I gave up and started spinning my pink mini-golf ball on top of the table. Watching it go around and around reminded me of the way it felt to travel between worlds. Funny how I'd always hated that feeling, and now I kind of missed it.

I realized the boys at the table were glaring at me for making so much noise with the ball. "Sorry," I said, slipping it back in my pocket.

I glanced across the cafeteria at Trish and Melissa. If I could manage to have an actual conversation with Aunt Evie, maybe I could patch things up with my ex-best friends too.

I got up and went over to where Trish and Melissa were hunched over a gossip magazine, pointing and giggling. "Hi, guys," I said.

"What do you want?" said Trish, glaring up at me.

"I know I already apologized for lying to you, but I wanted a chance to explain what happened." Neither of them said anything, so I kept talking. "It's just that I was embarrassed by how weird my family is, and I didn't want anyone to find out the truth. I felt really bad lying to you. I promise I will never do it again."

Trish and Melissa exchanged looks. Then they huddled together and whispered for a minute.

"Okay, we'll forgive you on one condition," said Melissa.

"You have to fix us up with Prince Lamb," said Trish.

I stared at them. "Both of you?"

"That's right," they said in unison.

They had to be kidding. My friends might have changed over the years, but they hadn't completely lost their minds. Had they? "But you can't both date him," I finally said.

"Why not?" Trish demanded.

"What's wrong with us?" said Melissa.

"Nothing. It's just—"

"It's my hair, isn't it?" said Trish, running her hand over her perfect curls.

"What? No!"

"Then what?" said Melissa. She gasped. "Did you tell him about my mole?"

"What mole?" But I didn't hear the answer because just then a loud *Pop!* echoed throughout the cafeteria.

I whirled around, praying it had just been a giant balloon exploding. But the sight of two oversized frogs in capes confirmed my fears.

Everyone watched as the two frogs hopped across the cafeteria, their necks bulging and their mouths calling: "Mistress Jenny? Mistress Jenny? Are you here?"

"What are those?" a girl shrieked.

"Evil alien frogs!" someone else cried.

Without thinking, I whipped off my backpack, scooped up the two frogs, and dumped them inside. Then I practically ran for the door. "Have to go fix these windup toys," I said loudly as all eyes in the cafeteria focused on me. "Aren't they so lifelike?"

I darted through the hallway and into an empty classroom. When I opened the bag, the two frogs leaped out.

"Are you two crazy?" I cried. "Do you want the Committee to turn everyone in my school into mindless zombies?"

"Mistress, we've been looking for you everywhere," said Crong. "You and the prince are in grave danger!"

"What are you talking about?"

"We don't have a lot of time," said Ribba. "He could be listening."

"Who?"

"Klarr!" the frogs said in unison.

"What? He's *here*?" I spun around, expecting to see the sorcerer's laughing eyes staring back at me. No one was there. Still, I had the crazy urge to dive under one of the desks and stay there forever.

"We got word that he discovered Prince Lamb was sent to your world," said Crong. "It will only be a matter of time before Klarr tries to kidnap him again."

"I just saw Prince Lamb," I said. "But we should go check on him." Before I could move a muscle, a chorus of screams echoed in the hallway.

"A monster!" someone cried out. "There's a flying monster attacking the school!"

I almost laughed. Of course there was. Why wouldn't there be? I grabbed one of the frogs in each hand and darted toward the cafeteria. Most of the students were pressed up against the windows, staring at whatever was outside.

"Go find the prince," I whispered to Ribba before putting her down on the floor. Then, still holding Crong, I pushed through the crowd and out onto the athletic field behind the school.

It was true that there was a monster, but it wasn't exactly attacking the school.

"Halga!" Crong said with a gasp.

I stopped in the middle of the field and watched as Halga circled high above us. Her wings reflected the sunlight like two giant mirrors. She looked terrifying from the ground as she wove in and out of the clouds. Then Halga's voice came down from the sky.

"Crong, we have to talk about this! It's not what you think!"

Crong jumped out of my hand and started to hop away in a huff.

Meanwhile, my classmates were running for their lives. Even some of the teachers were hiding under picnic tables. I didn't know how the Committee would deal with this, but I had to get Halga out of sight before the entire town saw her.

"Crong!" I said. "Get back here."

The frog turned around and shook his head. "I am not speaking to that beast."

"If you don't get her to come down, this entire place is going to get dosed with memory dust."

"That is not my concern," he said. "I am not the one making a scene."

"Crong, it's just a misunderstanding! I would never do that to you," called Halga.

"Do what?" I asked the frog. "Why are you mad at her?"

Crong crossed his tiny arms in front of his chest. "I saw her making eyes at one of the guards in the dungeon. I never thought she'd be drawn to a suit of armor, no matter how shiny it was!"

"Do you mean one of Klarr's guinea-pig guards?" I asked, choking down a laugh. "I don't think anyone could be crazy enough to be interested in one of them."

"That's not what it looked like," said Crong, turning away.

As Halga flew past again, I wanted to scream. After everything I'd done to try to make my life ordinary again, it was all falling apart in one day. But I couldn't just stand by and watch things spiral even more out of control.

"Crong," I said. "Can you make something to magnify my voice, so Halga can hear me?"

"I can try." He waved his green hands. Instantly, I felt my throat tingling.

"Hello?" My voice rang out across the entire field as if it were coming out of a speaker. Every pair of eyes focused on me. Even the kids still inside the school turned to stare at me through the windows. "Halga," I called up to the sky. "You have to come down."

"Not until I speak to Crong!" She swooped past, and I could see the stubborn look on her face. This was not going to be easy.

"You can't talk to him from up there," I said. "Come down."

"No," said Halga. "I won't set foot on ground again until he knows the truth."

"And what's that?"

"That I'm sorry he got the wrong idea, but nothing happened."

This felt like one of my adventures all over again. Getting creatures to make up or admit how they felt. Apparently, I just couldn't get away from situations that needed me to get involved.

"Halga, do you love Crong?" I called.

The beast swooped down again, and a giant tear rolled off her cheek. It landed on top of a picnic table with a loud splat. The teachers hiding under the table darted out from under it like beetles and scuttled behind the bleachers.

"Of course I love him!" cried Halga.

"Well, love means never having to say you're sorry." I clapped my hand over my mouth. That wasn't just a cheesy line that could have come out of a movie. It was actually *from* a movie, one of Aunt Evie's favorites. Apparently, I just couldn't stop myself.

Halga's face softened, and she let out something that sounded like a whimper. A moment later I saw a shadow at my feet. Crong was standing there, his eyes filled with tears.

"You are right, Mistress Jenny," he said. "I have been acting like a fool."

Then, with a wave of his hand, Crong lifted off the ground and flew into the sky to meet Halga among the clouds. A few gasps came from the crowd at the sight of the flying frog. Then there were some sounds of confusion when Crong threw his tiny arms around Halga's face and gave the corner of her lip a passionate kiss. Finally, the crowd groaned in disgust as Halga and Crong sank back to the ground, still locked in a slobbery smooch.

"Get a room!" one of the kids shouted.

As the happy couple landed, I marched over to them. "Okay, break it up," I whispered, though my voice still carried across the field.

"Thank you, Jenny," said Halga. "You really are a hero."

She reached out a front leg, and I saw my mother's purple bracelet dangling from one of her claws.

"What—?"

"Take it," said Halga. "It's yours. Crong can give me all the jewelry I want, but this belongs to you." She pushed the bracelet into my hand before I could object and turned back to Crong with a dreamy smile.

I stared down at the sparkling gems. I had thought I'd never see them again. Maybe having the bracelet back meant I'd finally have some luck. I gave it a squeeze and slipped it onto my wrist.

It was only then that I noticed the deafening silence.

Hundreds of eyes were staring at me. There was no way I could cover up everything that had happened. The Committee would hear about Halga's appearance and wipe everyone's memories, no matter what the side effects were. That didn't seem fair. The kids and teachers couldn't help what they'd seen. They had just been spectators.

That gave me an idea.

"Okay, everyone," I called, my voice still amplified for all to hear. "That's a wrap! Shooting of the film ends next month, and you should expect to see it in theaters early next year."

There was an uncertain silence. Then the crowd erupted in whispers. "They're making a movie?" I heard a few people say as some of the panic on their faces started to fade.

"You've all been a terrific audience," I continued. "Give yourselves a round of applause!" I started to clap loudly. The students and teachers glanced around at each other, still hesitant. "Come on. Don't be shy!"

Crong and Halga started clapping along with me, and soon most of the crowd had joined in. I could even see a few people smiling.

"Okay, now everyone clear out!" I said. "The crew has to strike the set!"

The clapping died down, and the crowd started to break up.

"I knew it wasn't real," I heard someone say. I sighed with relief before motioning for Crong to cut out the bull-horn effect. The frog waved his hands, and I felt the same tingling as before.

"Thank you, Jenny," said Crong. "You always know how to save the day!"

"Forget that," I said. "We have to find Prince Lamb before Klarr does."

Crong's face grew serious. "You're right." He turned to Halga. "Go back to our kingdom, dearest. I'll be there as soon as I can." He gave her a smooch, then another, and another.

I was just about to break up the lovefest, when I heard someone calling my name.

"Jenny, is that you?"

I turned to see Trish and Melissa slowly walking toward me.

"It *is* you!" cried Melissa. She ran up and threw her arms around my neck. A second later, Trish did the same.

"We thought we'd never see you again!" said Trish, finally letting go. Her voice sounded lower, as if the squeaky toy in her throat was gone.

"Where have you been for the past two years?" asked Melissa. It was the first time in a long time that I'd seen something besides emptiness in her eyes.

"Two years?" I said. And then I remembered what Dr. Bradley had told me, that a sudden shock might reverse the memory-dust spell. Seeing Halga must have done the trick. It had brought my friends' memories back!

The two girls stared at me, waiting for an explanation.

"It's a long story," I said with a laugh. "But you don't know how happy I am to see you guys!"

"We have so much catching up to do," said Trish as she linked her arm through mine.

Melissa grabbed my other arm and gave it a warm squeeze. "I didn't realize you were working on movies."

"Those puppets look so real," said Trish, eyeing Halga and Crong.

I glanced over at the two lovebirds, and reality came rushing back. "I'm sorry," I told my friends. "I have to go."

"What? But you just got here," said Melissa.

"I know. But don't worry, I'll be back soon! I promise!"

"Jenny!" Trish objected.

"I'll explain everything when I get back." Only after I'd said it did I remember that I wouldn't be able to tell my friends anything without risking having their memories erased again. But I'd have to worry about that later. For now, at least, it was good to know that I finally had my friends back.

I marched over and wrestled Crong away from Halga. "We need to go find Prince Lamb."

Crong gave Halga one last longing glance before he jumped up onto my hand. I pushed through the crowd, searching for any sign of the prince. Finally, I spotted a couple of Prince Lamb's popular friends hanging out by the edge of the field. I put Crong behind my back and went toward them.

"Hi, Jenny," one of the boys said, giving me a shy smile.

"Have any of you seen Prince?" I said, surprised they were actually giving me the time of day.

The boys shook their heads. "Next time you're working on a movie, do you think we could be in it?" another one asked.

Ugh. *That* was why they were talking to me now. I shook my head and rushed off.

"Bye, Jenny!" a couple of the boys called after me. I didn't care about silly boys when Prince Lamb could be in danger. I went back into the cafeteria and scanned the clusters of people.

"Look!" said Crong, pointing to a trash can nearby. Ribba was perched on top, her head in her tiny hands. She was shaking with croaking sobs.

"Ribba, are you okay?" I asked.

"I was too late," she cried. "He's gone! Klarr already got to him."

"He took the prince? How do you know?"

Ribba pointed to a nearby table. In the middle sat a shining red balloon. It had been twisted and tied into the shape of a tiny lamb.

Chapter 18

My head was throbbing as I stumbled out of the school with the frogs perched on my shoulders. Klarr had Prince Lamb. I had to do something, but what?

"We must bring you to the kingdom of Klarr immediately," said Crong, "so you can finally defeat the sorcerer."

"With what army?" I said. "If you haven't noticed, my big weapon is saying cheesy things. It's not like I can do magic or anything. There's no way I can defeat Klarr."

"There are other ways to take down a sorcerer besides magic," said a voice from behind me.

I froze. I knew that voice, but it couldn't be. "Dr. Bradley?"

There stood the doctor on the school steps, a big toothy grin on his face. I had never been so relieved to see someone. I wanted to tell him how sorry I was about everything, but his eyes sparkled back at me, telling me he understood. All that silly stuff I'd said to Halga about love earlier seemed to really be true.

"What are you doing here?" I asked him.

"The Committee said there was an emergency on your world." He glanced around. "But I see you took care of it all by yourself."

"I did the best I could. And I had some help."

"You never give yourself enough credit, Jenny," said Dr. Bradley. "I'm afraid that's been the trouble from the beginning."

"And you always give me too much. Half the time I just mess things up and wind up almost having my head burned off or getting stabbed by unicorns."

"Stabbed by unicorns?" said Ribba. "But that's great!"

I looked down at her in surprise. "What are you talking about?"

"I wish I could have been honest with you, Jenny," said Dr. Bradley. "But the Committee insisted that I let you learn things on your own."

"What do you mean?"

Dr. Bradley sighed and adjusted his glasses. "Those unicorns weren't trying to hurt you. They were trying to thank you."

"Thank me?" I echoed. "But they stuck me with their horns! They ran after me and tried to trample me!"

"That's what unicorns do," said Ribba. "They show their appreciation with little love jabs."

Dr. Bradley nodded. "So you didn't fail, Jenny. You taught the unicorns about sharing, just like you were asked to. Over the past three years, you've accomplished more than most adventurers do in a decade."

I couldn't believe it. After all of that, those stupid unicorns had actually been trying to be nice? "But why didn't Anthony tell me?"

"Maybe we should let him answer that himself," said Dr. Bradley, looking over my shoulder.

I turned to see a familiar, round face staring back at me. After all that had happened, I didn't feel an ounce of anger at the gnome anymore. Maybe he hadn't been the friend I'd always wanted, but he didn't deserve how I'd treated him. "I'm sorry I called you an elf," I said finally. "I didn't mean it."

"No, *I'm* sorry," said Anthony, and for once he wasn't grinning from ear to ear. "I know I wasn't always the best guide. I guess it was because I figured you could take care of yourself. The truth is, you didn't need me at all. You've done great on your own."

"You see, Jenny," said Dr. Bradley, coming up beside me. "You may not have mastered magic, but you make people feel safe. You come up with solutions when they can't see them on their own. That's what makes you an adventurer. Without the skills of your people, the magical worlds would have perished long ago."

It seemed strange to think that all my Hallmark card sayings and kindergarten lessons had made any difference. But I had to admit that they did seem to work pretty well in the magical worlds, even if I didn't understand why. All I had to do was say things like "Mind your manners!" and "It's all fun and games until someone gets hurt!" and everything tended to fall into place.

And the more time I spent in the regular world, the more I realized that I actually *liked* being an adventurer. When Halga and the frogs had appeared in my school and everything had gone into crisis mode, I'd been totally in my element. Maybe life as an adventurer wasn't perfect, but I'd missed it. Being a normal girl wasn't enough for me, not when adventuring was in my blood.

But no matter what kind of blood I had, it wouldn't be enough to defeat Klarr. The sorcerer was the most power-ful enemy I had ever gone up against. He didn't just scare me—he made me want to go hide under my bed with a teddy bear. But I couldn't let him win. Not anymore.

"Crong, do you think you can get the League together?" I asked.

The frog stood up tall. "Of course, Mistress, but what would you like us to do?"

"We're going to storm Klarr's castle."

"Hooray!" said Ribba, clapping her hands. "I knew you wouldn't let us down."

I turned back to Crong. "Can you have the League meet us there?"

"You can count on it," said the frog before disappearing with a determined *Pop!*

"Does this mean you have a plan of attack?" Dr. Bradley asked.

I wished I could say I did, but the truth was I had no idea what I was going to do. All I knew was that I couldn't let Klarr harm Prince Lamb. "I'm not sure," I admitted. "But if I really am the right person for this job, I guess I'll figure it out. Will you keep an eye on my aunt until I get back?"

"Of course I'll watch over your aunt," Dr. Bradley said. "And I will keep an eye on you too. But I'm sure you'll do splendidly, just like always."

"Thanks." I turned to Anthony. "Do you want to come with us?"

Anthony grinned. "Absolutely! I want to be there when you save the day." He took a step forward and lowered his voice to a whisper. "By the way, I worked out a deal with the Committee so that your friends won't get dosed with any more memory dust. You can tell them about your adventures as long as they swear never to tell anyone else."

I was stunned. That was the first time Anthony had ever done anything truly nice for me. Maybe he really did care. "Thank you," I finally whispered.

"It wasn't a big deal," Anthony said with a shrug. "I just had to promise to deliver some candy to the Committee every once in a while. Turns out the old crones love Tootsie Rolls."

I smiled. I couldn't wait to get back and tell Melissa and Trish about everything that had happened. If I made it back...

"All right, Jenny-girl," said Anthony. "Are you ready to go take care of that crazy clown?"

I swallowed. Was I ready? Yes. This was what I was born for. It was time to be an adventurer again.

"Let's go!"

Chapter 19

Ribba, Anthony, and I materialized behind a patch of trees just outside Klarr's castle. I was ready for a fight, but the coast was clear. Crong and the League were nowhere in sight, which meant we had to wait. I hoped they'd hurry up and get here soon. Now that I was at Klarr's castle again, I could feel the panic brewing in the pit of my stomach. I needed a plan. Some way to rescue the prince and to defeat Klarr for good. Then I'd never have to see that clown's face again.

I replayed what Prince Lamb had said to me ages ago, about seeing Klarr's moment of weakness. But what had caused it? I went over the events in my head again and again. Klarr had been attacking me, then Anthony had popped in and showered him with circus peanuts. But no, Klarr had winced in pain before then. It had been when…when Anthony laughed!

My mind started spinning. Was it possible? Was laughter his weakness? Maybe that's why he hated mouths so much. A clown hating laughter was ironic, but Klarr wasn't exactly the happy kind of clown. In fact, everything he did was intended to make others miserable. Maybe laughter really *was* his weakness.

Okay, my theory was a long shot. But it was the best I had to go on.

There was a loud *Pop!* and Crong appeared, surrounded by a dozen other creatures of various shapes and sizes, about half of them with mouths. They all bowed when they saw me. Even Ribba bowed at my feet, which made my cheeks burn. It wasn't like I was royalty or anything.

"All right, everyone. Gather 'round," I said.

The members of the League huddled up like I was a coach and they were waiting for me to psych them up for the big game. All we needed were some cheerleaders. Or at least a couple of pom-poms.

"Tell us what you need us to do, Mistress," said Crong.

Ready or not, it was game time. "First, we need to get inside the castle." I turned to Anthony. "Do you think you can blast open the door?"

"Easy peasy," he said.

"Then, I'll need the League to fight off any guards so we can try to get into the castle. Once we find Klarr, we're going to form a circle around him, and then those of you without mouths will try to deflect his magic. While those of you with mouths…will help me laugh in his face."

There were a few murmurs and concerned looks among the League members as Crong hopped toward me. "I'm sorry, Mistress. Did you just say that we're going to *laugh* at Klarr?"

"I think it's the only way to defeat him," I said, not mentioning that I could be completely wrong. If laughter turned out to be a huge mistake, we'd just have to find another way to beat him. Or lose all of our mouths, and maybe our lives, in the process. But it was better not to think about that.

The League still looked skeptical until finally Ribba jumped forward and said, "Jenny is the best adventurer there is. If she says it's the only way, then we do it."

That seemed to reassure everyone. I could have kissed Ribba's slimy head, but I settled for giving her a grateful smile.

"Okay," I said. "Everyone come up with something funny to think about, something that's guaranteed to make you laugh." The League members looked deep in thought. I tried to come up with a funny memory or image, but all I could think about was that first day when I'd arrived in Speak and seen hundreds of its mouthless citizens staring back at me with their hopeful eyes. I couldn't let them all down, not again.

"All right, let's go," I said. I had the two frogs jump onto my shoulders, and then I got into position. The League members gathered around Anthony, ready to strike with their magic. There was an earsplitting *Pop!* and the castle door shattered into a billion pieces.

We ran out from behind the trees and charged toward the hole where the door had been. Almost instantly, energy beams started flying toward us as dozens of animal guards poured out through the entrance. Anthony led the way, magic flying from his hands, while the frogs and I stayed behind him.

As we got closer, three figures emerged from the entrance, and I only needed a second to recognize them as my favorite trio of guinea pigs. Their eyes widened when they caught sight of me.

"No!" I heard one of them say.

"Not you again!" said the second.

"Why can't you just leave us alone?" asked the third.

The three guards looked at each other. Then they let out high-pitched squeals, threw down their weapons, and scampered away. In a moment, they had disappeared into the woods.

If only the sight of me was enough to scare off *all* the guards!

As Anthony and I got closer to the incinerated door, more and more of Klarr's guards fell around us, the League's magic putting them into a deep sleep. We might have been outnumbered, but the League members were determined. After all those years of living under Klarr's spell, they were ready to be done with him once and for all. And so was I.

We finally fought our way into the castle and charged down a long corridor. It was lined with colorful, striped fabric and smelled like popcorn. From somewhere deep inside the castle, I could hear faint circus music. It had to be part of Klarr's act, the one he'd tortured Prince Lamb and the other prisoners with.

"Go toward the music!" I yelled just before we hit yet another wave of guards and even more energy beams shot toward us. I shrieked as one of them whizzed past my head, singeing off a clump of hair. At least it hadn't been my head. Even Ribba's styling skills couldn't cover up something like that.

We went down one corridor after the next, the music getting louder. There were so many guards that I was starting to wonder if we'd make it, but the League didn't back down. Crong was zapping guards left and right, and even Ribba, who had never seemed all that magical, was conjuring up swarms of flies and shooting them at the guards' eyes.

Finally, I spotted a big wooden door at the very end of the corridor. The music was coming from behind it. More than a dozen guards were clustered in front of the door, clearly frightened but willing to go down with the ship. I guess none of them wanted to face Klarr if they failed to protect him.

"How are we going to get through all those guards?" I said.

"Don't worry, Jenny-girl!" said Anthony. "I'll get us inside. Just stay behind me."

The gnome let out a cry and charged forward, energy beams blasting from his hands. I darted after him, the frogs still on my shoulders. Guards fell around us as Anthony managed to clear a path to the door.

When we finally reached the doorway, Anthony pushed me behind him to protect me. And that's when I heard the loudest *Zap!* in the world, like ten different energy beams coming together. The beams hit Anthony right in the chest, and he let out a stunned cry. He stumbled backward, almost knocking into me, before falling forward onto the floor.

"Anthony!" I cried.

I started to kneel down to see if he was all right, but Crong's voice stopped me: "There's no time, Mistress! We have to go on. The rest of the League will stay behind to keep the guards back."

I realized that only a handful of the League members were still with us, most of them without mouths. The rest must have either fallen back or been knocked out. Behind me, the music throbbed through the door. How could we defeat Klarr with only me and the frogs to challenge him? But Crong was right. If we didn't go ahead now, we'd lose our chance. The battle would be over. I had no choice but to leave Anthony behind and hope he was all right.

"Okay, let's go!" I said.

Ribba and Crong stayed rooted to my shoulders, deflecting energy beams, while I turned and heaved open the door. A wave of music rushed at my face, making me stumble back. I forced myself onward and slammed the door shut behind me. The sounds of battle faded, replaced by blaring horns and deep drums.

We were inside a giant, circular room that looked just like the inside of a circus tent. On the edge of the ring was an invisible band, with horns and cymbals and flutes all playing themselves. There were no seats or bleachers, only a huge red chair in the center of the ring. And in the chair was Klarr, his eyes focused upward. I realized he was looking at a lone figure dangling from a trapeze, its hands bound together. It was Prince Lamb.

The sorcerer's eyes swung toward us, and the music came to a sudden stop. With a crash, the cymbals and trumpets fell to the floor. And then there was silence.

Chapter 20

Steady, I told myself as I stared into Klarr's terrifying face. *You can do this.*

The clown got up from his giant chair and took an enormous step forward. One of his red shoes crushed a balloon in his path, making it explode with a deafening pop.

"Release the prince!" I demanded, trying to keep my voice from shaking.

Klarr's painted-on smile stretched from ear to ear as he grabbed something from his pocket.

"He's got a poison flower!" said Ribba.

It was time. I started to laugh as loud as I could, thinking of any funny thing I could imagine: Prince Lamb impressing the boys at my school by eating napkins, Aunt Evie tickling the angry duck in our kitchen, and the totally terrified looks on my teachers' faces when they'd seen Halga swooping above our school. None of those things had seemed funny at the time, but now I was practically crying as I thought about them again. Ribba and Crong joined in, their froggy laughter echoing alongside mine.

The poison flower fell from Klarr's hand and landed on the dirt floor. He clapped his oversized hands over his large ears, trying to block the sound. Encouraged, I laughed even louder, laughing not only at memories but at myself. I'd been so afraid of this silly clown, and all along he could've been defeated by something so simple.

Klarr doubled over.

"It's working!" Ribba cried.

And in that moment, everything shifted. Klarr straightened up, as if he'd gotten a burst of energy. Ribba started to laugh again, louder than ever, but it was too late. We'd given him a second to gather his strength, and that was all he'd needed.

Tears were streaming down my face and my stomach was aching, but the laughter wasn't working anymore. Even though Klarr was still clearly in pain, he was moving toward us again, step by step. His eyes were murderous slits.

I stumbled back, still trying to laugh, but it was no use.

Klarr lifted his hands, and I knew what was coming. He was going to paralyze and torture me again. I wanted to turn and run, but I made myself stand my ground. I wasn't going to leave Prince Lamb behind.

Klarr's fingers began to glow, and I braced myself for the worst.

But at that moment Prince Lamb let out a battle cry, swung himself off the trapeze, and landed right on top of Klarr's head. The sorcerer staggered back in surprise. He tried to swat the prince away with his giant hands, but Prince Lamb managed to hang on to Klarr's curly wig.

Before I could do anything to help, Crong tore past me and charged at Klarr, energy beams flying out of his hands. But even though the sorcerer was distracted, he waved his arm and a thick beam of energy shot out of his fingertips. Crong fell to the ground without a sound.

"No!" Ribba and I both cried as we ran to the frog. I turned him over and was relieved to see he was still breathing. He was knocked out but all in one piece.

"Help!" Prince Lamb suddenly cried.

Klarr had finally managed to pluck the prince off of his head. He was holding Prince Lamb upside down and trying to shoot energy beams at him with his free hand.

"Get away from him!" I yelled, but that only made Klarr shoot at me instead. Ribba and I dove behind the giant chair as the beam hurled past us.

"What are we going to do?" asked Ribba.

I peeked out from behind the chair and saw the prince duck out of the way of another energy beam. It scorched the curved wall instead. The prince swung his leg out and tried to kick at Klarr's head, but he only managed to make contact with Klarr's giant red nose.

Prince Lamb's eyes widened. "Jenny, look!" he cried.

I leaned forward and saw that not only had Klarr's nose been knocked out of place, but that there was something underneath.

I stared in disbelief.

Where Klarr's nose had been was a big, gaping hole. All this time the clown's red nose had been covering up a misplaced mouth!

The sorcerer stood frozen, as if he couldn't believe his secret had been uncovered.

But I was anything but frozen, because everything finally clicked into place. It was just like in mini-golf! To win the game, you had to get the ball into the clown's mouth.

"Ribba, I need your help," I said, pulling my trusty pink

mini-golf ball from my pocket. "I need you to infuse this ball with laughter."

The frog's eyes widened. "You need me to *what*?"

"It's the only way we can defeat Klarr. Use your magic to put my laughter into this ball."

"But I don't have that kind of power!" said Ribba. "Crong's the one—"

"Crong is unconscious. It's up to you. You have to at least try."

Ribba nodded, but she still looked terrified. "If you laugh...I might be able to capture it."

I couldn't think of a single funny thing, but I made myself fake the heartiest laugh I could. Ribba waved her tiny arms, and the air in front of my mouth started to glow. Then she pointed her hands toward the pink ball and held them there.

I waited for the ball to start glowing too, but nothing happened.

"It's not working!" I said. Maybe my fake laughter was the problem.

"Let me try again," said Ribba. This time, she looked more confident. "Give me another laugh."

I heard Prince Lamb cry out, and I knew we didn't have much time. I closed my eyes and the image of the citizens of Speak floated into my head again. And all of a sudden, I realized how hilarious it had been. All those eyes staring back at me, all those empty spots where mouths should have been. It was so totally creepy! And I'd had to stand there with a *frog* in my mouth, trying not to scream or cry or laugh, and act like this kind of thing happened to me all the time. I started laughing so hard, my stomach felt like it was spasming.

When I couldn't giggle a second longer, I opened my eyes and saw that the laughter was glowing in front of my face like it was on fire. Ribba waved her small hands, and this time the glowing laughter started to weave itself into the ball. It wrapped around it like a cocoon and slowly settled into all the tiny pink holes.

Ribba fell back on the ground and the glow disappeared. "It's done," she said, panting. Clearly, the magic had taken a lot out of her.

I grabbed the ball, and it made my fingers tingle with warmth. I was ready to jump out from behind the chair when I realized I didn't have a club to hit the ball with. My mind swirled, trying to find a solution. Crong was still unconscious, and Ribba was too weak to conjure anything. No one else had the magic to do it.

Wait!

I suddenly realized that Dr. Bradley had to be watching us on his puddle screen, just like he always did on my adventures.

"Dr. Bradley!" I cried. "If you can hear me, I need your help! I need you to send me your cane!"

Nothing happened. Prince Lamb let out another cry, and I knew I was running out of time. If I didn't have a club, I'd have to throw the ball at the clown and hope I didn't miss.

But then, something by my feet started to glow. *Pop!* Dr. Bradley's wooden cane appeared on the ground.

"Thank you!" I cried to the air. I should have known the doctor would come through.

I didn't waste another second. I leaped out from behind the chair and ran over to where Klarr and Prince Lamb were still in the middle of a wrestling match. When Klarr saw me, he threw the prince on the ground and started to stomp my way. I should have been terrified, but this time I was determined. I wasn't going to let this clown mess with me anymore.

I placed the ball on the ground, wound up, and swung the cane with perfect form. The end of the cane connected with the pink ball, and it sailed through the air. All that practice had really paid off. My aim was dead-on. Before Klarr could duck out of the way, the ball went straight into his nose hole.

Hole in one.

For a second, nothing happened. Klarr only straightened up, a surprised look on his face. Then his skin started to change. It shrunk and shriveled like it was being sucked inward. His eyes went cross-eyed, and his grin turned more and more into a frown. From deep inside of him came the sounds of laughs and giggles and chuckles. They grew louder and louder and louder until—

BAM!

There was an earth-shattering explosion, and I was thrown to the ground. Almost instantly, what seemed like bucket-loads of confetti started to rain down all around me.

And then everything was silent.

I looked around for any signs of Klarr, but the ground near the trapeze was empty except for the confetti still falling from the ceiling. The only thing I could see in the dirt was my trusty mini-golf ball. When I picked it up, it was so hot that it almost burned my hand.

Still in shock, I went to untie Prince Lamb. "Are you all right?" I said. "Are you hurt?"

"A little bruised but okay," he said, grinning. "I knew you could defeat him!"

I couldn't believe it. Was Klarr really gone? I glanced around again, expecting to see him charging toward me, but nothing was there.

"We're really safe, thanks to you," said the prince. "This means I can finally go home!"

I looked at him. "Do you mean you want to come back to your world?"

"Of course I do," said Prince Lamb, smoothing his hair into place.

"But wouldn't you rather stay in my world and be popular? If you come back here, you'll have to be a prince again."

Prince Lamb smiled. "Jenny, being popular has been absolute torture. People hang on my every word even more than when I was a prince. I would gladly give it up."

"What? But if you hated being popular, why did you do it?"

Prince Lamb blushed. "To impress you, of course. Ribba told me that girls only like popular boys."

I almost swallowed my tongue. Prince Lamb had done all of that to impress me? I didn't know if I should be flattered or amused, so I settled for a bit of both. "Thanks."

"Jenny?" a thin voice asked from somewhere nearby. It was Ribba. She still looked pale and weak, but she was also smiling. "Crong's waking up."

As if on cue, Crong lifted his head and looked around. "What happened?"

"Jenny did it!" Prince Lamb said, beaming.

Crong blinked and slowly sat up. "Is Klarr...?"

"He's gone," said Ribba, her eyes shining with tears.

I nodded, the truth finally sinking in. "It's over. We defeated him."

"*You* defeated him," said Prince Lamb.

"If you hadn't knocked off his nose, and if Ribba hadn't worked her magic, and if Dr. Bradley hadn't sent me his cane, we'd all be in Klarr's trapeze act by now," I said. "It was a team effort."

It was really over. After everything, I'd never have to worry about being attacked by an evil clown again. I let out a long sigh. I felt like I'd been holding my breath for weeks.

Suddenly, the door to the chamber burst open. I spun

around, ready to fight whatever guards were headed our way. But I almost fell over with relief when I saw Anthony grinning back at me.

"You're okay!" I ran over and gave him a bone-crushing hug.

Anthony chuckled as he hugged me back. "Of course I'm okay. I just took a little snooze, that's all."

"You were amazing," I said. "The way you charged those guards. We couldn't have gotten to Klarr without you." For the first time ever, I was proud to call Anthony my guide.

He shrugged one of his shoulders. "I had to work off all those calories somehow, didn't I?" He popped a gum ball into his mouth and looked up at the last few pieces of confetti falling from the ceiling. "You did pretty good yourself, Jenny-girl. Seems we were right about you being the one to defeat that ridiculous clown."

"What about the guards?" I asked.

"They surrendered to us. Turns out they weren't big Klarr fans either. It looks like we have ourselves a good, old-fashioned victory."

I started to ask about the prisoners in the dungeon but was cut off by a strange sound all around us, like the air rushing out of a balloon. When I glanced up, I saw that the ceiling was sagging.

"The castle's deflating," I said. "Quick, we have to get out of here!"

I herded everyone out into the hall and back through the maze of corridors as the walls started coming down all around us. We managed to make it outside before the main entrance began to collapse.

I was glad to see that the other League members had made it to safety and were helping the last of the prisoners out of the dungeon as the castle's stone walls started to sag and buckle. Even the towers were shrinking. Now that Klarr was gone, his castle was disappearing with him.

As I watched in fascination, something moved near the castle entrance. It was one of the dancing bear statues. At first I thought it was also deflating. Then I realized that the stone was actually falling away, revealing something else inside.

I ran over and spotted a teenage girl curled up on the base of the statue. Her eyes were closed and she was very pale, but I was relieved to see she was only in a deep sleep. The other three bear statues were also crumbling, revealing two sleeping teenage boys and another girl.

"The other adventurers!" I said.

"What?" said Prince Lamb, coming up beside me.

"The ones who disappeared. They were here the whole time. Klarr turned them into statues."

I couldn't believe it. For years I'd dreamed of meeting other adventurers like me. Once they woke up, I would finally have my chance. Maybe things weren't as hopeless as I had been making them out to be. If I could meet other adventurers, maybe that meant I could find my parents one day too.

As I stood there grinning like a fool, I felt something nudge my hand. I looked down to see a woolly head at my side. It belonged to a small white lamb.

I gasped. "Prince Lamb, is that you?"

"It is indeed," said the lamb. "I guess Klarr's magic has finally worn off."

Despite his curly hair and his wide dark eyes, I could see something of the human boy he'd been moments earlier. "Are you okay?" I asked.

Prince Lamb looked down and examined his four legs. Then his sheep mouth stretched into a smile. "I'm better than okay. I finally feel like me again!"

"Wait," I said. "If Klarr's magic is gone, does that mean the Silence spell is over?"

"Look!" said Ribba, pointing.

The dozens of creatures who'd escaped Klarr's prison were milling around, looking shocked and overjoyed at the same time. Every single one of them had a mouth.

"It's true!" cried Crong. "The Silence is over!"

I couldn't believe it. I'd done it. As much as I hated to admit it, the Committee had been right. I *had* been the one for the job.

"Jenny the Adventurer," said Prince Lamb. His voice was loud and official. "We are grateful to you for your help. You have done this land a great service." He gave me a deep bow.

My cheeks burned. "It wasn't just me. It was all of us."

"Our kingdom cannot even begin to show you our gratitude," he continued. "But we shall give you whatever reward we can. Any jewels or treasure you desire."

I glanced over at the frogs and Anthony, who were all beaming at me with pride. As I ran my fingers over my mother's bracelet, I had to admit that helping magical kingdoms did feel really good. My parents had been adventurers, and I was meant to be one too. I smiled.

"Thank you, Your Highness," I said. "But I have all the treasure I need." I paused, unable to believe what my tongue wanted to say next. But I realized it wasn't any chip in my head urging me to say it. The Committee had nothing to do with it at all. It was just how I really felt. "Friendship is the best reward."

Acknowledgments

What are you doing reading the acknowledgments? Don't you think Jenny would roll her eyes if she saw you looking at a list of cheesy, sentimental stuff? But even she would have to admit that sometimes a heartfelt thank-you is in order, so here we go:

To Ray Brierly for being an awesome husband, best friend, and first reader.

To my amazing family and friends for a lifetime of love and support.

To my critique partners—Sheryl DePaolo, Anne Handley, Megan Kudrolli, and Alisa Libby—for letting me know when I'm on the right track and not being afraid to tell me to start all over.

To my fabulous agent, Ammi-Joan Paquette, for an unlimited supply of wisdom and enthusiasm.

To Rebecca Frazer, Aubrey Poole, and the rest of

the Sourcebooks team for taking a chance on my wacky little book.

To the Associates of the Boston Public Library for giving me the opportunity to call myself a real writer and to the PEN New England Discovery Award committee for reassuring me that I was on the right path.

To the faculty, students, and friends at Simmons College for continuing to challenge and inspire me.

And to all the writers, readers, librarians, booksellers, and bloggers who make the children's book community such a rewarding place.

About the Author

Born in Poland and raised in the United States, Anna Staniszewski grew up loving stories in both Polish and English. After studying theater at Sarah Lawrence College, she attended Simmons College where she earned an MA in Children's Literature and an MFA in Writing for Children. She was named the 2006–2007 Writer-in-Residence at the Boston Public Library and a winner of the 2009 PEN New England Susan P. Bloom Discovery Award. Currently, Anna lives outside of Boston, Massachusetts, with her husband and their adopted black Labrador, Emma. When she's not writing, Anna spends her time teaching, reading, and challenging unicorns to games of hopscotch. You can visit her at www.annastan.com.